KARIN ALVTEGEN is regarded as one of the most exciting new crime writers in Scandinavia. *Missing* was awarded the premier Scandinavian crime writing award and was also nominated for the Poloni Award and Best Crime Novel 2000 in Sweden. It is currently being translated into sixteen languages. Alvtegen lives in Stockholm.

ANNA PATERSON has worked as a literary translator from the Germanic languages for over a decade. She won the prestigious Bernard Shaw Prize for Literary Translation in 2000.

MISSING

Karin Alvtegen

*Translated from the Swedish by
Anna Paterson*

CANONGATE

First published in Great Britain in 2003
by Canongate Books Ltd,
14 High Street, Edinburgh EH1 1TE.
Originally published in Sweden as *Saknad* in 2000 by
Natur och Kultur, Stockholm

This edition published in 2004

10 9 8 7 6 5 4 3 2 1

The publishers gratefully acknowledge general subsidy
from the Scottish Arts Council towards the Canongate
International series.

British Library Cataloguing-in-Publication Data
A catalogue record for this book is available on
request from the British Library

ISBN 1 84195 498 5

Typeset by Palimpsest Book Production Limited,
Polmont, Stirlingshire
Printed and bound in Denmark by
Nørhaven Paperback A/S

www.canongate.net

*A*s the servants of Christ and as guardians of God's secrets, thus should we be seen and understood. Nothing more than fidelity can be demanded of such a guardian. For me, it is as nothing if mankind or any of its courts of justice should decide to condemn me, nor do I sit in judgement over myself. Indeed, I know myself to be truly without guilt, but this alone is not sufficient justification for what I do. The Lord will judge me.

No one must sit in judgement before the right time, when the Lord comes. He shall force that which has been hidden in darkness to emerge into His light and He shall make known all councils of the heart.

Then God will praise each one as he or she deserves.

Thank you Lord for my courage. You have listened to me, heard my prayers and directed me on the right path.

Let me be Your instrument. Let me execute the sentences due to those who have sinned.

Let my beloved meet with You and be with You always.

Then will my hope return.

Then will I find peace.

The green suit had a classy label and no one who looked her over could have guessed that it cost less than one hundred kronor at Oxfam. The waist button on the skirt had been replaced by a safety-pin, but no one would notice.

She called the waiter and asked for another glass of white wine.

One empty table away, tonight's target was sitting on his own. She hadn't begun her act and wasn't yet able to judge how aware he was of her.

He was just getting on with his starter.

There was plenty of time.

She swallowed a mouthful of wine from her refilled glass. The wine was dry, cool to perfection and probably quite expensive. She had no idea of the price. It didn't matter.

She looked at her man surreptitiously and felt, rather than saw, that he was staring at her. Over the edge of the wine glass, she let her glance swivel in his direction and meet his, but then, marking mild disinterest, she allowed it to wander across the room.

The Grand Hotel's French dining-room was really a magnificent place. She had been there three times before, but tonight had to be the last visit for a while. Pity, because they put out fresh fruit in the bedrooms. The towels were exceptionally thick and laid on in such quantity that it seemed risk-free to let a couple slip into your briefcase.

Still, it was unwise to challenge fate. It would be a disaster if the staff recognised her.

He was looking at her again, she could sense it. She quickly pulled out her diary from the briefcase, checking today's date. How irritating . . . Impatiently, she tapped on the table-top with her immaculate red nails. Two different meetings at the same time – how could she have allowed herself to be double-booked? Worse, with two of her largest customers!

She observed him out of the corner of her eye. He was still watching.

A waiter walked past her table and she hailed him.

'You wouldn't have a phone I could borrow, please?'

'Of course, madam.'

She kept following the waiter with her eyes as he walked over to the bar counter, returning to her table with a cordless phone.

'There you are, madam. Please dial nine to get a line.'

'Thank you.'

4

She leafed through her diary to find the right number before dialling.

'Hallo, this is Caroline Fors, my company is Swedish Laval Separator. I'm so sorry but I've managed to get myself snarled up tomorrow morning – a double booking. I just wanted you to know that I'll be with you, but about two hours later than we agreed.'

'*Twenty, twenty-five and thirty. Pip.*'

'Good. I'll be there as soon as I can. Bye for now.'

She sighed and wrote *salamiwurst 14.00 hours* on the line just below *basement flat* and closed her diary.

By chance their eyes met just at the moment she took another drink from her wine glass. She felt sure of his complete attention by now.

He smiled at her.

'Got a problem?'

She too smiled but shrugged her shoulders, a little embarrassed.

'Easily done,' he said sympathetically, looking her over. He was edging close to her carefully positioned bait now.

'Are you alone or are you waiting for someone?'

His eyes were fixed on her.

'No, I just liked the idea of a glass of wine or two before going back to my room. It's been a long day.'

She picked up her diary and put it into

5

her briefcase. This was it, nearly done. She would hook him soon. When she had replaced her briefcase on the floor, she saw him pushing away his emptied plate and raising his glass to her.

'Would you mind if I joined you?'

Already – and she had barely begun her fishing trip. With a little smile, she got ready to beach her catch. She mustn't be too quick, though. Playing hard to get for a while always worked a treat. She hesitated for a couple of seconds before answering his question.

'That would be nice, but I'm really about to call it a day.'

He rose, picked up his wine glass and sat down opposite her.

'I'm Jörgen Grundberg. Pleased to meet you.'

He held out his hand to her, she shook it and introduced herself.

'Caroline Fors.'

'That's a lovely name for a lovely lady. I'd drink to that.'

On his left hand a thin wedding ring caught the light.

'Cheers.'

The waiter was bringing Mr Grundberg's main course, but stopped short when he realised that his guest had gone away. Jörgen Grundberg waved to him.

'Here I am. The view's better from over here, don't you agree?'

Her smile was rather forced, but happily Mr Grundberg did not seem particularly sensitive to people's feelings.

A white plate with a silver cover was put down on the table between them. He shook open the decoratively folded linen napkin and draped it over his lap. Then he rubbed his hands together. This guy clearly enjoyed his food.

'Aren't you going to eat anything?'

She could feel her stomach rumbling with hunger.

'No, I don't think so.'

He lifted the silver lid and a gorgeous smell of garlic and rosemary wound its way into her nostrils. She could feel saliva filling her mouth.

'Come on, of course you must have something to eat.'

He wasn't looking at her now. Instead he was focusing his attention on the delicate operation of cutting pieces off the fillet of lamb.

'You must eat to keep up your strength,' he said, moving a laden forkful towards his mouth. 'Didn't you learn that at your mother's knee?'

As likely as not, her mother had said so and much else besides. That alone was a good reason for declining. But by now she was really very hungry and the bowl of fruit in her room did not seem so tempting any more.

While he was chewing, he called the waiter who came immediately, but was kept standing by until Grundberg had finished his mouthful of food.

'Another one of these for the lady. Charge it to room 407.'

He smiled at her and waved his key-card in front of the waiter.

'Room 407.' The man went away.

'I hope you don't mind?'

'I'm perfectly able to pay for my own food, you know.'

'Of course you are. I just thought I'd better pay to make up for being so pushy.'

With pleasure, to be sure.

She drank some more wine. The guy was almost too good to be true. Ran on autopilot. There he sat, chomping away at his lamb fillets, totally absorbed by the food as far as she could see. In fact, for the moment he seemed to have forgotten that he had company at the table.

She observed him. About fifty years old, she guessed. His suit was expensive and since he'd just ordered two meals, without a second thought, even though it was the Grand's French dining-room, his bank balance must be more than favourable.

Good. He was perfect.

He looked as if he was used to eating well. His neck wouldn't stay contained inside his collar and had oozed outside it at a point just above the knot on his tie.

Overall, his appearance might have deceived an untrained eye, but she was far too acute: he was obviously an upstart. For one thing, his table manners told even a casual observer that no one had spent much time teaching him how to eat politely. No one had tapped his elbow when he let it rest on the table and no one had taken the trouble to tell him off for putting the knife in his mouth.

Lucky him.

He was actually using the first-course cutlery for his main course.

He had almost finished by the time her plate arrived. The waiter removed the silver cover and she had to use quite a lot of will power not to follow Jörgen Grundberg's example and go all out for the food. She cut off a small piece of fillet and chewed it carefully. Meanwhile he shamelessly used the blade of his knife to scrape up the last dribble of sauce and transfer it to his mouth. She swallowed.

'This is really very good. Many thanks.'

'You're welcome.'

He burped, trying to conceal it behind his napkin, and pushed his plate away. Then he pulled a blister-pack from a white medical-looking box, squeezing out one capsule. He swallowed it with a gulp of wine.

'Well, now, "Swedish Laval Separator" – that's quite something.'

He put the box back in his pocket, and she

carried on eating, but shrugged her shoulders lightly. This bit was always tricky.

'What about you? What do you do?'

She couldn't believe how well this worked, every time. Maybe all men in expensive suits are clones of the same ancient forefather. As soon as a man in a halfway decent career was given a chance to speak about his own successes, he would forget everything that seemed to have interested him just minutes earlier.

'Import trade. Mostly in electronics. I check out new gizmos and if I believe in them, I buy the rights and start up production in Latvia and Lithuania. You'd be surprised, but production costs can be reduced by up to two-thirds if one only . . .'

He was happily rabbiting on about his brilliant business ideas. All she needed to do was look at him and nod at regular intervals. She was enjoying her meal, letting garlic and rosemary absorb her mind fully.

When her plate was empty and she looked up at him again, she realised he had stopped talking. Now he was watching her. High time to start with stage two. She had half a glass of wine waiting, but it couldn't be helped.

'That was wonderful. Thank you so much.'

'You were quite hungry after all, weren't you?'

She put her knife and fork down on the plate. At least someone at this table had been taught how to signal the end of a meal correctly.

He seemed ridiculously pleased with himself, smiling contentedly.

'Working out what a woman really needs is one of my specialities.'

She wondered if that held true for his wife as well. Then she folded her napkin.

'It's a shame, but now it's definitely time for me to say goodnight. Thank you again, both for the pleasant company and the nice meal.'

'I'd like to tempt you to share a little night-cap upstairs.'

His eyes met hers over the edge of the glass.

'I appreciate the offer, but no, I can't. I've got a long day ahead tomorrow.' Before he could stop her she waved to the waiter, who responded instantly.

'My bill, please,' she said.

The waiter bowed politely and began clearing the table. He eyed Grundberg's crossed knife and fork.

'Have you finished, sir?'

The barely audible irony in his voice made her hide a smile in her wine glass, but it was lost on Grundberg, who merely nodded without spotting the barb.

'Now, you must let me pay for this. That's what we agreed.'

He tried to put his hand over hers but she pulled it away in time.

'I must pay for my wine, though.'

The waiter left. She took hold of her hand-bag, which had been hanging over the back of her chair.

He didn't want to back down.

'No, don't think of it. No arguments now.'

'Thank you – but you can't really stop me, you know.'

He had begun to irritate her and she had sounded more aloof than she intended. Grund-berg was smiling at her. This was the wrong time to cool his ardour and so she smiled back at him. She put her handbag on her knees and opened it to find her wallet. It didn't take long to search the two compartments.

'Oh God, no!'

'What's the matter?'

'My wallet's gone.'

She rooted in her handbag again, frantically. Then she hid her face in her left hand and sighed deeply.

'Take it easy now. Are you sure it couldn't be in your briefcase?'

She allowed this suggestion to sink in, giving both of them, especially him, new hope. Then she put the briefcase on her lap. He couldn't see what was inside, which was just as well. He might have been troubled to find that Caroline Fors had nothing in her briefcase except her diary, a pack of frankfurters and a Swiss army knife.

'No, it isn't here either. Oh God! Someone must have stolen it.'

'Now, now. You must take it easy. I'm sure all this can be fixed easily enough.'

The waiter returned with two bills on a small silver tray, and Grundberg hurriedly produced his American Express card.

'Take both off this.'

The waiter looked at her to get permission and she nodded briefly. He turned and left.

'I'll pay you back as soon as I . . .'

'No problem. Don't worry about a thing.'

She hid her face behind her hand again.

'And I had my hotel voucher in the wallet. Dear God, I haven't even got a room. This is terrible.' She placed a lot of emphasis on the last bit. Abjectly, she shook her head.

'You must let me help. Just you stay here and I'll have a word with the reception people.'

'But I couldn't possibly ask you to . . .'

'Of course you can. We'll deal with anything that needs settling once you've sorted out the business with your lost wallet. No hurry at all. Now, you just sit back and relax. I'll see to this.'

He got up and went off to the reception desk.

She drank some wine. Cheers!

In the lift, and then all the way to her room, she almost went over the top with gratitude. He had brought two shots of whisky and, outside her door, made one final attempt.

'Sure you haven't regretted saying no to that night-cap?'

This time he even winked at her.

'It's sweet of you, but I must get on the phone at once. I've got to cancel my cards and put a stop on the accounts.'

Even to him, this was an acceptable reason. He gave her one of the glasses of whisky and sighed.

'What a shame.'

'Some other time, perhaps.'

He sniffed a little and produced her keycard. She took it from him.

'Truly I'm so very grateful.'

She wanted to get into that room quickly now and put the card into the slit in the door. He put his hand on top of hers.

'I'm in 407, remember. You know where I am if you change your mind. I'm a light sleeper.'

He didn't give up easily. Gently, using all the self-control she could muster, she pulled his hand away.

'I won't forget.'

The card didn't work. The lock-release click didn't happen. She tried again. He smiled.

'Goodness. You must have got my card. Who knows, maybe it's an omen?'

She turned and looked at him.

He was holding her card between thumb and

index finger. She felt an unmistakable wave of bad temper mounting inside her. She took the plastic card from him and put his into his jacket pocket. Her door opened easily this time.

'Good night.'

She stepped into her room and began pulling the door to. He stood there looking at her like a disappointed kid. No sweeties after all. And he had been exceptionally decent to her, it must be said. Maybe he deserved at least a little something to cheer him up. She lowered her voice.

'I'll be in touch if I begin to feel lonely.'

His face lit up like a sun and with that sight facing her she finally closed the door and locked it from the inside.

Have a nice life.

She couldn't wait to get her wig off. Then she opened both the bath-tub taps full on. Her scalp was itching and she leaned forward, running her fingers through her hair. When she straightened up, she observed her face in the mirror.

Life had left its marks. She was only thirty-two, but could easily have been ten years older. That would actually have been her own guess. Many disappointments had etched a fine mesh of wrinkles round her eyes, but she was still good-looking. Or, at least, good-looking enough to attract men like Jörgen Grundberg, and she aspired to nothing more.

The tub had filled almost to the brim and when she lowered herself into the hot water, some of it was slopping over the side. She reached over the edge to try to save her suit, which she'd let drop on the bathroom floor. Instead, her movement set up a wave-motion and more water spilled onto the floor. She would have to try to dry the suit on the hot towel-rail.

She leaned back, enjoying the bath. This was the kind of thing that gave life meaning. If one's ambitions were modest, that is. At least living out of a rucksack had taught her to appreciate the small things in life that others took so much for granted. Lots of people didn't even notice many simple sources of pleasure.

Once, she too had led that kind of life, so she knew what she was talking about. Though it was getting to be a long time ago.

She had been Miss Sibylla Wilhelmina Beatrice Forsenström, the Chief Executive's daughter. That Sibylla had had a bath every day, as a matter of course, as if it had been a human right. Maybe it should be. Still, it had taken losing the opportunity to make her value the whole experience.

Sibylla Wilhelmina Beatrice Forsenström.

It wasn't so strange that she'd never managed to fit in. She had been given a life-long handicap as a christening gift.

Sibylla.

Even the dullest of the children in Hultaryd's school reached unexpected intellectual heights in their efforts to invent new rhymes on her name. It didn't help that the Burgers 'n' Bangers stall in the main square had the same name and helpfully drew attention to it by displaying 'Sibylla' on a back-lit sign. This added sausages – and many rude variants – to the range of useful allusions to build jokes round. When it got out that she was called Wilhelmina Beatrice as well, everyone's imagination seemed to know no bounds.

Our child is unique! No doubt. But then, aren't all children?

Her parents' stratagem worked on one level at least. In spite of their daughter spending years in the local school, which was full of common children from the lower classes, there wasn't the slightest risk of her getting mixed up with them.

Sibylla's mother had always made a point of emphasising how special her daughter was, which of course gave Sibylla's schoolmates every justification for ostracising her. It mattered very much to Beatrice Forsenström that Sibylla should know her position in the social hierarchy, but it mattered even more that everyone else should know it too. Nothing had any real worth to her, unless others valued it too and preferably found it very desirable. Beatrice derived her greatest pleasure from arousing admiration and envy.

Almost all the parents of her fellow pupils were working in her father's factory. Mr Forsenström was a leading member of the Local Council and his pronouncements weighed heavily. Most of the jobs and much else in Hultaryd depended on his say-so and all the children knew this. On the other hand, they were too young to be serious about the employment market and anyway most of them hoped for more in life than stepping into their parents' shoes. They didn't want to spend their lives minding a machine at Forsenström's Metal Foundry and felt they could get away with a bit of name-calling in the school corridors.

Not that Mr Forsenström cared one way or the other.

Managing the successful family firm kept him very busy. He had no time to concern himself with bringing up children and he wasn't interested anyway. The excellent carpets in the Forsenström mansion showed no trace of a path beaten by him to Sibylla's room. He left for work in the morning and came back in the evening. He ate at the same dining table, but was often engrossed in thought or checking through accounts and other documents. Sibylla never had a clue about what went on behind his correct façade. She just finished her food properly, leaving the table as soon as she was given permission.

'Very well, Sibylla. You may go to bed now.'

Sibylla rose and reached for her plate to take it to the kitchen.

'Sibylla, please. Gun-Britt will clear the table later.'

But at school they always had to tidy up after their meals. It was really hard to remember which rules to follow there and which ones applied at home. She left the plate where it was and went over to her father.

'Good night, Daddy.' She kissed him quickly on the cheek.

'Good night.'

Sibylla walked towards the door.

'Sibylla. Haven't you forgotten something?'

She turned and looked at her mother.

'Aren't you coming upstairs to say good night?'

'Really, darling. It's Wednesday. You know tonight is a Ladies' Club meeting. When will you learn?'

'I'm sorry.'

Sibylla went to her mother and kissed her too quickly on the cheek. It smelled of powder and day-old perfume.

'If there's anything you need, ask Gun-Britt.'

Gun-Britt was the maid. She took over when Mrs Forsenström didn't have time to cook or clean or help Sibylla with her homework. Goodness gracious, she had to think of her charity work, after all. Without Mrs Forsenström, how would the little children in Biafra fare?

Sibylla remembered envying these far-away children, who were so scared and upset that nice ladies from the other side of the Earth spent their time worrying about them. When she was six years old, she felt she'd better do something to make herself more interesting: becoming just as scared as these other children seemed a good idea so she decided to sleep one night in the large, dark and spooky attic in their house. She took her pillow, tiptoed up the stairs and went to sleep on a pile of old rugs. Gun-Britt found her there in the morning and had to tell on her to Beatrice, of course. The recriminations took more than an hour and the scene got on Beatrice's nerves so badly that she had a migraine attack that lasted for several days afterwards. This was Sibylla's fault, of course.

There was at least one thing she could thank her mother for. After almost eighteen years in the Forsenström home, she had developed an almost uncanny ability to analyse the mental states of people around her. Sheer instinct for self-preservation had attuned her to respond to the slightest shifts like a living seismograph, always alert to her mother's every whim and quick to predict likely causes of bad temper. She remained remarkably sensitive to the body language and verbal signals of people around her. This, as it happened, was of great help in the life she'd ended up leading.

The water in the tub was getting cool. She got out, shaking off drops of water and all these memories too. A beautifully thick, soft dressing-gown was hanging over the heated towel-rail next to the tub, and she wrapped herself in it and went to inspect her room. There was an American soap on the TV. It was accompanied by lots of canned laughter but turned out to be really funny. She settled down to watch it for a while, carefully going through her nail-varnishing routine in the meantime.

Always clean and tidy – Rule Number One.

Sticking to this rule set her apart from most other homeless people she knew. Being aware of it had allowed her to take one step away from the kind of misery that crushes all hope.

What mattered was *what you looked like*. As simple as that.

Respect was the preserve of people who appeared to live by the social norms – the citizens who didn't differ too much from the rest. If you didn't manage to fit in, you were treated accordingly. Weakness is a provocation in itself. People are scared silly when confronted with others without pride. Shameless behaviour is an affront. Surely no one would behave like that unless they deserved to be what they were? Everyone has a choice, so what's your problem? Do you like wallowing in your own shit? Fine, but don't expect other people to care.

Not to care, maybe, but if you're good you might get a cut from the taxes we pay, beggar's alms so that you don't actually starve to death. We're not monsters, you know. Month after month, we keep shelling out to help types like you. But don't imagine it means that you can hang around our underground stations and shove your filthy hands under our noses to demand still more cash handouts. It's a fucking awkward imposition, you know.

We mind our own business – how about you minding yours? If you've got any complaints about what's done for you, we suggest you sod off and get a job. No place to stay? Get real – do you think a good fairy brought us our homes? Besides, if it's such a problem, how about us building an institution to house people like you? No drifting about any more.

Not near my place of course. No way. Got the children to think of, you know. The last thing we need are a lot of useless junkies hanging out in our neighbourhoods, stealing and shooting up and losing syringes all over the place. Somewhere else, by all means.

She rubbed herself all over with white skin lotion and looked longingly at the bed. Still, it was wonderful just sitting here, warm and clean, knowing a soft, inviting bed was waiting for her. She would be able to sleep undisturbed the whole night through.

She decided to stay up to enjoy the anticipation of it for a little longer.

M y mother knew that I was different from the others. She always feared the times when I might be disappointed. If I wanted something very much, she would try to prepare me for what failure could do to me. She tried to make me lower my expectations in order to save me from pain.

But if all ventures include preparing for failure, then not succeeding will finally become a goal. I cannot live like that any more.

Not now.

Rune was all I ever wanted. I had always been hoping to meet someone like him and then, suddenly, there he was. He came to mean more to me than life itself.

How many times have I asked You to let me know if that was why I had to be punished?

Lord, did our carnal lust cause us to sin so gravely that You could not overlook it and instead take pleasure in our love for each other? You took him away from me, but You never welcomed him into Your realm.

I have asked You, God: what must be done that he should be forgiven?

For when a Will exists, it is first necessary to show that the testator has died. Death alone can validate the Will. And the contrary is true, for as long as the testator lives, his Will is invalid. Hence the previous relationship must be celebrated in blood, for according to the Law, all can be purified by blood and also, until blood has been shed, there can be no forgiveness.

Lord, I give thanks to You for making me understand what I must do.

S he woke when someone knocked hard on the door. Instantly awake, she got up and started to look for her clothes.

Shit, how could she have slept in? The clock radio showed quarter to nine. The burning question was: had Grundberg figured out by now that he had been tricked or had he just woken up with a particularly urgent hard-on?

'One moment!'

She hurried into the toilet and grabbed her clothes.

'Hallo there. Open the door, please. We've got some questions to ask you.'

Damnation. It wasn't Grundberg, but some woman. Had one of the hotel staff recognised her, in spite of the wig?

Oh, fucking hell.

'I'm not dressed yet.'

Silence in the corridor. She hurried over to the window and looked out. No get-away route there.

'This is the police. Please hurry up.'

Police! Now what the fuck?

26

'Ready as soon as I can. Just give me a couple of minutes.'

She put her ear to the door and heard steps walking away. There was a laminated chart showing emergency exits right in front of her nose and she studied the options while she fumbled with the safety-pin in the waistband. Checking the number of her room, she found that it was just two doors away from the emergency stairs. She rushed to get her jacket and handbag, and then listened again at the chink in the door. Cautiously, she opened the door a fraction and peeped into the corridor. It was empty.

She stepped briskly into the corridor, shutting the door behind her quietly. Seconds later, she was running down the back stairs. They had to lead to a door opening into the street.

Then she remembered. The briefcase! She had left it behind. It pulled her up short, but it took only a moment of hesitation to realise her briefcase was lost. And so was the wig in the bathroom. Shit, almost 740 kronor down the toilet and such a brilliant investment too, which should have given her many nights of undisturbed sleep. Even the complimentary soaps and the little shampoo bottles had been forgotten.

At the bottom of the stairs she stopped in front of a metal door with a lit green Emergency Exit sign. Pushing on the locking bar, she opened the door enough to put her head outside. A police car was parked just twenty-odd yards away, but it was empty and this gave her enough courage to step out into the street. She looked around, realising that she was at the back of the Grand Hotel.

The morning traffic in Stall Street had come to a standstill. She squeezed between the cars without looking too obviously stressed and crossed Blasieholm Square. At the Arsenal Street corner, she turned right, walked past Bern's Café and down Hamn Street. No one seemed to have followed her, but to make sure she continued across Normalm Square, along Bibliotek Street and began slowing down only when she was outside the Wiener Café.

The café seemed a good place to sit down and think. She chose a table as far away from the window as possible and tried to calm down.

This had been a far closer shave than at any other time since she'd started to spoil herself with nights in hotels. She had better forget about the Grand for quite a while. What she didn't understand was how Grundberg could have got wise to her. Had any of the staff recognised her and phoned his room? Why in that case leave her in peace all night? Well, she'd never know. Perhaps just as well.

She looked around the café. Everywhere, people were having breakfast.

She wished she had some money. A drink

would have been nice, her throat felt sore. She wondered if she was running a temperature as well and put her hand to her forehead. Hard to tell.

She looked at her watch to check the date. It had stopped again. She'd worn it on her arm ever since receiving it as a Confirmation gift seventeen years ago. A present from mummy and daddy. With best wishes for a happy, prosperous life.

Imagine that.

It was true that she was happier nowadays, relatively speaking. She had decided to make something of her miserable life and had come to believe she actually could do it. This was important, but anyway she was much happier in her present life than as the well-behaved daughter from a solid, middle-class home. 'Good' behaviour had been the first thing to go and, come to think of it, it was hard to say why they tolerated it. As if that wasn't bad enough, many other character flaws were discovered and finally all family patience with her ran out. That was the end of her life in the executive villa.

The one reminder of her past came in the form of a white envelope without a return address that turned up in her box at the Drottning Street post office every month, year in and year out. It always contained exactly one thousand five hundred kronor.

Never a word in writing, never any questions

about how she was getting on. Her mother paid to clear her conscience, just as she'd paid to stop herself worrying about the little children in Biafra. As likely as not, her father knew nothing about it.

Renting the post office box cost sixty-two kronor a month.

A young waitress with a ring in her nose came to her table and asked what she'd like to order. Quite a few things actually, if only she'd had the money. She shook her head, got up and started walking down Bibliotek Street towards the Central Station. She had to change her clothes.

Halfway across Normalm Square she saw it. A bright yellow poster on the newspaper kiosk screamed the big news in bold capitals. She had to read it three times before she finally realised the implications for her.

NEWSFLASH!
BESTIAL MURDER LAST NIGHT AT GRAND HOTEL
TT News Agency, Stockholm

Late last night a man was murdered in his bedroom at Stockholm's Grand Hotel. He was travelling on business, away from his home in central Sweden and had been staying at the Grand for the last two nights. According to statements by staff, the man had intended to leave on Friday.

Police sources are refusing to disclose any detailed information about the murder at this stage, but have revealed that the body was found by hotel staff around midnight, after a guest had alerted them to the presence of bloody marks in the corridor outside the murdered man's room. The police also confirmed that the body had been subjected to some kind of mutilation. The police have no evidence pointing to the identity of the murderer at this stage, but expect that interviews with hotel staff and guests will help to clarify the events of the fatal evening. At the time of going to press, the police investigation at the site of the crime was not yet completed, and the Grand Hotel will stay closed to the public until further notice. This morning, the body will be subjected to a forensic examination at the Institute for Forensic Medicine in Solna. It is expected that interrogation of staff and guests should be completed at the end of today and access will then return to normal.

That was all, apart from a photo of the Grand covering a whole page.

The rest of the article listed other murders involving mutilation carried out in Sweden over the last ten years. It was lovingly illustrated with pictures of the victims, complete with their names and ages.

So that's why they had knocked on her door.

Thank God she'd got away. How could she have explained her presence in one of Stockholm's most expensive hotels? She couldn't afford to pay for a coffee in its Wiener Café. What hope had she of persuading them that she deserved a night in a proper bed now and then – even if always paid for by someone who could easily spare the cash? Nil, that's what. She wouldn't have stood a chance. No one would have understood, for none of them had ever led her kind of life.

'This is no fucking library, love. Do you want a paper or not?' The man in the kiosk was getting fed up. She didn't answer, just meekly put the paper back in the rack.

It was cold and she really did have a sore throat. She started walking towards Central Station again. She needed money and there were three days left until the next giro was due to arrive in her post box. In other words, she couldn't get at it until Monday.

There was a machine dispensing change in the Left Luggage facility at Central Station. She went there and stood in front of it pushing the note-feed button several times.

'What's wrong with this thing?'

She spoke loudly and distinctly so that no one in the vicinity would fail to realise how irritated she was. She pushed the button again a couple of times, then sighed heavily and looked about.

A man behind the deposit counter had noticed her and she walked over to him.

'What's the problem?' he asked.

'The machine doesn't work. It swallowed my hundred-kronor note without producing any change at all and my train's leaving in exactly eight minutes.'

The man opened his till. 'It's been playing up recently.'

That's a lucky break.

He counted out ten ten-kronor coins and put them in her hand. 'There, now. If you hurry you'll still catch your train.'

She smiled and put the money away in her handbag. 'Thanks ever so much.'

Luckily she had the key to the luggage locker in her jacket pocket, not in the briefcase she had forgotten at the Grand Hotel.

She collected her rucksack and, after a few minutes in the ladies' toilet, emerged wearing jeans and a padded anorak. She had decided what to do next.

It had to be a night with the Johanssons.

On her way to the allotments in Eriksdal she bought one tin of baked beans, a loaf of bread, a bottle of Coke, two apples and one tomato. She felt the first drops of rain just as she was crossing Eriksdal Street. For days now the sky had been covered by low cloud as grey as pewter.

All the allotment sheds seemed abandoned and she was grateful for the dull March day that did not tempt gardeners outdoors to their plots. Maybe it was just too early in the season anyway. The snow seemed to have gone for good this year, but the ground might still be hard with frost.

This was the first time she had gone there during the day, which was taking a risk, but she was tired and weary. She was running a temperature and needed peace and quiet.

As usual, the key was tucked away in the hanging basket. They had removed the geraniums that were flourishing in the basket every summer, but the key had remained in its old hiding place. It had been the obvious place to check when she turned up at the little cottage for the first time, almost five years ago.

Kurt and Birgit Johansson, the actual owners, had no idea they were sharing their cottage with Sibylla. She was always careful to leave it as she found it and never damage any of their things. She had picked their cottage partly because of finding the key so easily, but also because the cushions on their garden seats were unusually thick. Pushed together on the floor, they made a decent mattress. Besides, the Johanssons had the excellent sense to equip their small leisure hide-away with a paraffin heater and hotplate. With any luck, she would be left alone for a good while since they restricted their visiting to the summer months.

The cottage, really little more than a shed, was damp and cold. Still, the single room with a floor area of about ten square metres made it one of the biggest allotment buildings around. Along one of the walls stood a couple of kitchen cupboards, next to a small sink. She checked the cupboard under the sink for the bucket that should be in place under the cut-off drainpipe.

There was a small table with flaking paint near the window, which was partly covered by flyblown flowered curtains. Two odd wooden chairs were placed on either side of the table. She drew the curtains, took a wrought-iron candlestick down from a shelf and lit the candle. By now she was shivering.

She pulled up the zip on her anorak. The paraffin can was almost empty, so she'd have to walk to the garage and fill it up later in the afternoon. Once the heater was lit, she took a china bowl from a cupboard, placed her apples and tomato in it and put it on the table. She had learned to appreciate the small, good things in life, like making your surroundings look as nice as possible. She pulled her sleeping bag from the rucksack and lined up the seat-cushions on the floor. They were damp, so she put her mat down first. Then she crawled into the bag.

Resting her head on her arms, she studied the

ceiling panels and decided to forget all about the Grand Hotel. Nobody knew about her and even if someone had noticed her, they'd never be able to work out who she was. Feeling better now that she'd convinced herself she was safe, she began to descend deeply into sleep, untroubled by any dark premonitions.

As soon as she heard the brisk knock on the door, she knew who was on the other side.

She was in third form at the time. They were having a lesson in Geography. Everyone was staring at the classroom door.

'Come in.'

Miss put down her book and sighed when Beatrice Forsenström stepped in.

Sibylla shut her eyes.

She knew that Miss disliked these unannounced visits by Mrs Forsenström as much as Sibylla did herself. They were short but always broke the flow of the lesson and always involved some new demand for special treatment of Sibylla.

The issue this time was a plan to raise money by selling Christmas decorations. A group of parents had been making decorative wreaths and bouquets and the pupils in Sibylla's class were asked to be door-to-door sellers. The proceeds would help to pay for a school-trip in the spring.

Beatrice Forsenström had not joined the parent group. She had no patience with that kind of collective effort and the prospect of spending several evenings fiddling with folksy handicrafts was simply out of the question. Quite unsuitable for someone of her standing. Indeed, her reservations applied to her daughter, too. The child must not be expected to rush around knocking on doors asking for hand-outs like some little beggar. When Sibylla brought the note from school, Beatrice had crumpled it and thrown it into the wastepaper-basket.

Now, no one could miss the irritation in Mrs Forsenström's voice.

'So how much is each child expected to get from selling these things?'

Miss had gone to stand behind her desk.

'It depends. I'm not at all sure what the final sum will be.'

'Please let me know as soon as you have an idea. My daughter will not join in the selling, but naturally I'll make a financial contribution.'

Miss looked at Sibylla. She was focusing on the geography book in front of her. *There are four rivers in Halland County.* Then she heard how Miss tried her best.

'But the children are so looking forward to the selling part. They think it's really exciting.'

'Quite so, but you mustn't include Sibylla. Just tell me what would be appropriate and

38

'I'll give you the money there and then. Don't worry about that.'

'You must realise that we took this initiative precisely so that parents shouldn't have to pay extra for the school-trip.'

Suddenly Beatrice Forsenström looked pleased. Sibylla understood that her mother had manipulated Miss into saying exactly what she had hoped to hear. Now Mrs Forsenström took the chance to express her precise views on the whole matter.

Sibylla shut her eyes.

'Nothing personal, but I must say it seems extraordinary that the school should make decisions of this nature without consulting *all* the parents. I don't doubt that some of them thought this arrangement might be the best way to deal with their problems, but personally I prefer paying what's due as and when. Just do remember in future that my husband and I wish to be informed of anything involving our daughter. And of course, we expect to be listened to before any venture is agreed.'

Miss didn't say any more after that.

She had wanted to go selling with Erika. Miss had paired everybody off so that no one would go alone. Sibylla had been looking forward to it for a whole week. She heard her mother turn round and leave.

The first protests came the moment the door slammed shut.

'Miss. It isn't fair if Sibbie is excused from selling.'

'Miss. Can I go round with Susanne and Eva instead now?'

Erika had sounded hopeful.

Torbjörn who was sitting just in front of Sibylla turned round to her and said: 'If you've got such a lot of money your mum could pay for the whole class to go on the trip.'

She felt the tears burn behind her eyelids. There was nothing more hateful than suddenly being the target of everyone's eyes.

'Listen class, it's time to take a break now.'

The banging of chairs being pulled back. When Sibylla looked up again she was alone in the classroom. Only Miss was still there, standing behind her desk. She smiled wanly at Sibylla and sighed.

Sibylla felt something running out of her nose. She had to sniff to stop it from dripping on the desk.

'I'm really sorry, Sibylla. There's nothing I can do.'

Sibylla nodded and looked down again. The picture of the harbour fortress in Varberg became bubbly in two places when her eyes overflowed. Miss went over to her, putting her hand on Sibylla's shoulder.

'You can stay in this break, if you like.'

She felt quite dopey when she woke up. Must have been a bad dream. Her throat was swollen and it hurt to swallow. The heater had gone out and there was no more paraffin. She reached for her boots. They were freezing. A raw chill was spreading from the boots up through her legs. She was already wearing her anorak.

Lifting the hem of the curtain, she peered outside. The other allotments looked quiet and empty. She grabbed an apple on her way out and then opened the front door. It wasn't raining any more but the sky was such a dark grey it seemed strange that light could penetrate it at all.

The small garden had been neatly prepared for the winter months. The Johanssons had been very careful to follow recommendations in their gardening books. All dead plants had been cut back and put on the compost heap just inside the wooden fence. They had put fir branches over the borders, presumably where their most tender specimens were hidden during the winter.

'Are you looking for somebody?'

She started, turning quickly to see who had spoken. There was a man standing on the other side of the fence at a point outside the scanning range from her window. He was holding some cut branches.

'Oops! You really made me jump!'

He looked at her suspiciously and she couldn't blame him. It was well known that the Eriksdal Park area was frequented by junkies.

'Kurt and Birgit asked me to look after their cottage for a couple of weeks. They're off to the Canaries.'

She walked over to him and held out her hand across the fence. Maybe this chatty mention of the Canary Islands was a bit much? It was too late for second thoughts now.

'My name is Monica. I'm Birgit's niece.'

He shook her hand and introduced himself.

'Uno Hjelm. Sorry to bother you, but we operate a kind of Neighbourhood Watch here. There's quite a few weird characters about in this area.'

'I know. That's why they asked me to turn up once in a while to keep an eye on things.'

He nodded. She sensed that her lies had gone down quite well.

'Off to the Canaries, eh? That's something else, now. Didn't say a word about that last week.'

No surprise there.

'It was a sudden inspiration. Well, they came across a cheap offer.'

He looked towards the sky.

'Well, we can only hope they get better weather down there. Not such a bad idea, getting away to the sun for a bit.'

'I couldn't agree more.'

He seemed to be dreaming about travelling, so she took the opportunity to move on.

'I'll go for a walk now and come back later.'

'Right you are. Well, we might still be here, though I'm ready to give up pretty soon. I just thought I'd come and look the place over.'

She nodded and walked down the path towards the small gate. She only hoped that Kurt and Birgit wouldn't turn up while she was off to the Statoil garage.

Now, that would confuse Mr Hjelm.

She walked as quickly as she could. The label in the sleeping bag stated that it would protect against temperatures as low as fifteen degrees below zero, but she'd woken up feeling frozen after her brief nap. If only she had a couple of aspirins for her throat. Maybe she could scrounge some at the Salvation Army hostel?

She had almost reached the Statoil garage when the rain started again. Drying wet clothes was an utterly miserable exercise and she almost ran the last bit to get under the roof. If only she had an umbrella for the way back!

The news posters for that afternoon were on display outside the garage doors. She looked quickly at them in passing. One was yellow and the words were printed on two lines.

VICTIM OF RITUAL MURDER
AT THE GRAND
MYSTERIOUS WOMAN WANTED BY POLICE

She stopped to look.

There was a photo below the headline. No question whose face it showed.

It was Jörgen Grundberg's.

B eatrice Forsenström sounded disapproving.
'This is not the moment to discuss it. Just
put on your dress and get ready now.'

Sibylla was sitting on the edge of her bed in her
underwear. She'd been steeling herself, choosing
her moment with care. They were dressing for
the Christmas party at her father's firm, the
one time in the year when her mother might
be open to persuasion. The idea of the party
always put her in a good mood and she would
be full of anticipation, hurrying about trying to
get everyone looking their smartest. After all, in
little Hultaryd there were few other opportunities
for her to enjoy her status to the fullest.

'Please Mummy, I'd really like to go out
selling the Christmas things. Just one day.'

She'd tilted her head to the side appeal-
ingly. Maybe on this happy evening, her mother
would indulge her little daughter?

Beatrice was about to leave the room.

'Sibylla, don't forget to wear your black shoes.'

She swallowed. One more try. It couldn't do
any harm.

'Please Mummy . . .'

Beatrice stopped. Now there was a vertical crease between her eyebrows.

'Sibylla, you've heard me speak my mind already. My daughter doesn't have to run around begging to find the money for a school-trip. If you really insist on going, your father and I will pay whatever is required. It's quite wrong of you to make such a fuss and on this night of all times. You might show a little gratitude for what we do for you.'

She marched out of the room.

Staring at the floor, Sibylla was thinking that this was it. End of story. Not that she'd ever had a chance. Questioning her mother's decision had been too cheeky in the first place and now she'd only made it worse. Her mother had been jolted out of her party mood and Sibylla would be punished. Rows had to be paid for, over and over.

The outlook was Grim, as if things weren't bad enough already.

The Christmas party at Forsenström's Metal Foundry was a regular event. Sibylla had come to feel the same way about the Christmas do as she did about root canal fillings. Executive Director and Mrs Forsenström were showing off their seasonal benevolence by inviting all Foundry employees, complete with their spouses and children.

Sibylla's presence was a given, as was seating her at the high table for special guests. It was raised on a small platform and of course no other children were allowed to sit there. The young people had a table of their own, increasing the distance between them and Sibylla.

The dress spread out on the bed seemed to be mocking her.

It hadn't even occurred to her that she might be let off wearing that dress, never mind that she was twelve years old and all her mates would be in jeans and V-necked tops from Fruit of the Loom. That was neither here nor there for Granny had taken the trouble to go to one of the best shops in Stockholm and buy this dress for dear Sibylla. She would put it on and sit next to her parents on the podium, looking out over the people.

She pulled the dress over her head. Looking at herself in the mirror, she saw its little-girl bodice flattening her breasts, which had started growing at last. It felt really tight. It was going to be a dreadful evening.

Her mother was calling from downstairs.

'Get the two blue hair-grips. Gun-Britt will help you with them.'

An hour later, hairgrips in place, she was seated between the Sales Manager and his smelly wife. She answered their questions about school politely, but kept glancing at the 'young table'. Her mother's eyes had been wandering in her direction several times. Presumably she was brooding over how to punish her daughter for being so difficult. What would she do?

The answer didn't materialise until the dessert.

'Sibylla, won't you sing something for us?'

A black abyss opened up, right under her chair.

'Mummy, must I really?'

'Don't fuss, darling. You know so many nice Christmas songs!'

The Sales Manager was smiling ingratiatingly.

'A Christmas song would be a treat, just right for the occasion. Do you know *Shine Bright Star Above*?'

She was caught now. There was no escape. She glanced round the table, but everyone was beaming at her. Someone started to clap and the applause was spreading to all the tables. The young people turned their faces her way, starting to chorus 'Sibylla! Sibylla! Sibylla!' to make her stand up.

Beatrice sounded frosty.

'Now, we don't have to woo you any more than this, do we Sibylla? Everyone is waiting.'

Slowly she rose, pushing the chair back. The noisy room grew silent. She drew a deep breath. Get it over now. Someone at the young table shouted to her.

'We can't see you, stand on the chair!'

She stared in mute appeal at her mother, who just waved one hand a little to show she had no objection. Sibylla's legs were shaking so much, she feared she'd fall off the chair. The sneering looks on the faces of the young crowd were unmistakable. This was obviously the thrill of the evening. She inhaled deeply, starting to sing in a quavering voice.

Even before reaching the end of the first line, she realised that she had pitched the start far too high to manage the notes at the end. Right enough, she didn't and as her voice was faltering, barely suppressed laughter hit her like a whiplash. Blushing furiously, she sat down. After a few seconds, the Sales Manager started applauding and, hesitantly, others followed suit.

Meeting her mother's eyes, she saw that she had been punished enough. She'd be left alone for now.

On the way back, her father was pleased at the very satisfactory evening. Beatrice, leaning on his arm, was nodding in wifely agreement. Sibylla, walking a few paces behind them, had just decided to pick up a really nice stone when her mother turned her head.

'And your singing went perfectly well after all, didn't it?'

Neither of them missed the actual meaning of her words, but Beatrice couldn't resist another remark to round off her disciplinary exercise.

'Such a shame you lost control over your voice at the end.'

Sibylla didn't bother with the nice stone.

O f all the bloody awful fucking things to happen. He had seemed so perfect.

Her first reaction almost immediately gave way to the realisation that this time she'd really caught it. Obviously the police would be especially interested in the woman Grundberg had picked up, fed and then, always the gentleman, fixed a hotel room for as well.

It was pretty certain she was the mysterious woman the police were looking for. Worse, in the circumstances, no one would care to help her just for the asking, that much was certain too. Her first feeling was rage and she marched straight into the garage shop to pull a paper from the stand. The centrefold headline left no room for doubt.

MURDERER MUTILATED VICTIM.

Three words in heavy black type. Below, a full-page photograph of Jörgen Grundberg smiling broadly at the camera.

Unnamed sources alleged that the murderer had sliced open the dead man's torso and removed unspecified internal organs. The police admitted that some kind of religious symbol had been left at the scene of the crime, suggesting a ritual act of slaughter.

'Gruesome stuff, isn't it?'

Sibylla looked up. The man behind the counter nodded towards the paper.

'That's eight kronor for the paper, then. Is that all?'

She hesitated, fingering the coins in her pocket. Eight kronor was a lot to spend, just for a newspaper.

'A can of paraffin too, please.'

The man pointed for her to help herself from the right shelf. After paying, there were only nineteen kronor left in her purse.

Back at the allotments, Hjelm was no longer to be seen. She closed the door behind her and settled down with the paper. Reading the first four lines was enough to convince her that she was the wanted woman.

Who, the paper was asking, was Jörgen Grundberg's mysterious female companion, who had dined with him in the Grand's French restaurant? How had she managed to vanish in the morning, slipping unseen past the police cordons? The public was encouraged to contact the police headquarters with any information that might have a bearing on the case. The number to ring was displayed in large print.

She felt queasy. Seconds later she realised why. She was under threat.

What was she to do? The simplest answer was to ring that police number and explain the situation, insisting that she was innocent. The drawback was that she would have to let them know her personal details, including her ID number. A single computer check would tell them that she hardly had an official existence. This would instantly make them curious about her, the last thing she needed. Being left alone to mind her own business was all she ever wanted. She'd managed to do just that for fifteen years now. No one had chased her.

Of course she'd committed lots of minor illegal acts, misdemeanours that never harmed anyone poor or needy. She was not at all wicked but still, there were many things she'd rather not have the police look into. Living outside the margins of the normally acceptable for so long had shaped her. She was no longer in the system.

Being an outcast was part of how she lived, who she was. That she should be allowed to survive on her own terms seemed a small thing to ask, but she knew the media would turn the story of her life into something she couldn't endure. Not that she was proud of what she'd done so far, but anyone who tried interfering and laying down the law could go to hell.

No stranger would ever really understand why her life had turned out the way it had. Too bad if she'd been born with a silver spoon in her mouth. What had happened, had happened.

'Henry, I just can't take her with me. You know what it was like last time!'

Beatrice Forsenström was preparing for her annual visit to her mother and two aunts. Henry Forsenström didn't have much time for these ladies and the feeling was mutual. Beatrice went to see them on her own.

Sibylla had speculated about the possibility that once upon a time her mother really must have married her father for love because Beatrice's parents had been so opposed to the marriage. Beatrice's family was upper-class. Her parents, Mr and Mrs Hall, surveying the world from inside their huge apartment in Stockholm's prestigious Östermalm district, had dismissed the son of Forsenström's Foundry as 'not really one of us'. When anyone wanted to marry into the Hall family 'a good family background' was what really counted. 'New money' was automatically suspect.

Besides, what would a Hall girl do, buried in Hultaryd? No one had ever heard of this one-horse place somewhere in the Småland uplands. Still, it's your funeral, my dear, just don't come complaining to us afterwards.

Sibylla had picked this up gradually, listening to her mother's conversations with Granny at mealtimes. Apparently, Granny was also displeased at how long it had taken Beatrice and her husband to produce children. Displeased, though not at all surprised. What can you expect? Beatrice had been all of thirty-six when Sibylla was born.

Sibylla's grandmother had a finely honed ability to make herself understood, a skill relying entirely on insinuations and covert accusations. Her daughter had inherited it in full. As a grown-up, Sibylla had sometimes wondered if she too carried the same dissembling gene.

At that time, she had been a teenager and hiding halfway up the stairs to listen to what her parents were saying about going to see Granny.

'Her cousins simply can't understand what she's talking about half the time. They make fun of her. I shouldn't expose her to that.'

Henry Forsenström said nothing. Perhaps he was just looking through some of his documents.

'Her accent is even coarser than some of the working-class children here, you know.'

Her father sighed audibly, but must have felt he should comment.

'What's wrong wi' that. She's born 'n' bred in these parts after all.'

Henry Forsenström's version of the local dialect showed no regard for proper speech. Beatrice didn't answer at once. Although Sibylla couldn't see her, she felt she knew exactly what her mother's face looked like.

'Anyway, I think she'd better stay here this time . . . Besides, I'd have a chance to get out on my own for a change. Mummy mentioned a premiere at the opera on Friday – they're doing *La Traviata*.'

'You do as you think best, of course.'

Sibylla had never again been allowed to travel with her mother to Stockholm. The next time she arrived in the capital, it was under quite different circumstances.

When she woke the following morning, her body was telling her that all was not well. The little shed made her feel trapped. The paraffin heater had cut out and the air was cold. Her throat didn't feel quite as rough as it had, thank God. The night before it felt like a really bad throat infection, the kind you might need to take penicillin for. It's tricky to persuade a doctor to see you without being a registered patient and now it would be worse still, because she was presumably a wanted person.

She was hungry and ate the last piece of bread. There was nothing to drink because she'd finished the Coke at supper last night. She ate the tomato and the apple as well. Then she started packing her things.

She put away the iron candlestick and the fruit-bowl, stacked the cushions and finally looked around to check she hadn't forgotten anything. Swinging her rucksack onto her shoulder, with one hand on the door handle, she suddenly hesitated. It was a long time since she'd felt fearful.

Her rucksack was slipping off her shoulders. She shut the door again.

Bloody hell. Stay cool.

But she sank down on one of the kitchen chairs, leaning her head in her hands. As a rule, crying was not something she did because she knew only too well how pointless it was. For as long as she was left in peace to do her own thing, she normally never wanted to cry anyway. There was only one cause of grief that might still surface, although hidden so deep down in her mind that she only rarely became aware of the pain.

Her conscious thought was almost always focused on food for the day and sleeping quarters for the night ahead. Everything else was secondary.

She had her savings, too.

She put her hand to her chest, where the sacred 29,385 kronor were tucked away inside a safe purse, hanging on a strap round her neck underneath her clothes.

Soon she would have enough saved up. With this money she would finally reach the goal she had fought hard to achieve. Her decision to live differently one day had been utterly sincere and thinking about it had buoyed her up during the last five years. She wanted to change. Instead of always moving on, she wanted a country cottage to live in. It would be her home, where she could peacefully lead her life in her own way. Maybe she would grow vegetables, maybe keep some hens. Draw water from her own well. She didn't dream of comfort, just four walls that were hers alone.

Peace and quiet.

She had investigated and found that about 40,000 kronor would be enough, if you were prepared to live without electricity and running water in unglamorous countryside, somewhere obscure. That was exactly what she wanted. In the far north her kind of place might be even cheaper, but the thought of the long hard winters frightened her. She would keep struggling for a little longer instead.

During the last five years she'd put away as much as she possibly could of the monthly alms from her mother. Once in that purse the money simply didn't exist any more, no matter how cold or hungry she was.

Just a few more years and then she'd have enough . . .

She put the notes down on the table in front of her, arranging them in a star pattern. She always went to the bank to exchange the money she received for new crisp notes.

Notes that her mother had never touched.

After a while, looking at her money made her feel better again. It usually cheered her up. The next stage in recovering her fighting spirit would be a visit to an estate agent to keep informed about movements in house prices.

She gathered up her money, put it safely back in the purse, pushed the chair neatly back in place at the table and locked the door behind her. Her steps were lighter now.

She got as far as Ringen. A glance at one of the posters on the newspaper kiosk made her sense of calm evaporate. Now her problems were no longer about surviving for another day.

Now she was on the run.

WOMAN CHARGED WITH BUTCHERY MURDER.

That was the headline. There was a picture of a woman with a caption underneath naming her: Sibylla Forsenström, 32 years old.

'Dear Sibylla, don't look so sour. Please try to smile at least.'

Obedient as she was back then, she had tried. The effect was ghastly. Whatever she might have looked like seconds earlier, it couldn't have been worse than this. Even her mother presumably thought so, because she'd hidden the picture away until now. Curling tongs had been applied to her fringe, symmetrically on either side of the central parting, and the tips of the curls plastered against her temples. Her eyes had that unmistakable cowed look.

60

She was feeling nauseous now. Nineteen kronor left. The paper cost eight.

There has been a breakthrough in the investigation of the 'ritual slaughter' of Jörgen Grundberg (51) in his room at the Grand Hotel last night. A woman suspect, Sibylla Forsenström (32) is wanted by the police and has been formally charged in her absence. As *The Express* learned yesterday, this is the woman with whom the 51-year-old was seen on Thursday evening. The receptionist on duty that night has now told the police that Mr Grundberg himself booked a room for the woman, who gave what turned out to be a false name. The wanted woman managed to get through the police cordon early on Friday morning, leaving behind several articles including a wig that she allegedly wore the previous evening. The police also found a briefcase which, some sources suggest, may contain the murder weapon. The police are not prepared to reveal any details about the weapon. Fingerprints on the briefcase identified the woman as Sibylla Forsenström. The same prints were found on the key to the victim's room and in her hotel room, where a glass with the victim's prints was also found.

The police are baffled as to her whereabouts. In 1985 she escaped from a mental hospital in southern Sweden where she was an in-patient treated for psychological problems. Since then she has not been in contact with any state or local authority agency. No one seems to know anything about her life during the intervening fourteen years. Police records of her fingerprints were kept after an incident involving a car theft and illegal driving in 1984. Sibylla Forsenström grew up in a well-to-do family, based in a small industrial town in east Småland.

As she has been without a fixed address since 1985, the public are asked to let the police have any relevant information. However, the police also warn that she is likely to be confused and violent. Forensic psychologists, currently examining a diary found in her briefcase, claim that several notes are of a disturbed, incoherent character. The photograph, as the police are anxious to point out, is over sixteen years old. The waiter who served the woman and her alleged victim on Thursday evening described her as polite and well groomed. He is assisting a police artist with the creation of a more up-to-date image. Information about the wanted woman should be given to the police, either at the nearest police station or by phoning 08-401 0040.

She could feel the sick taste in her mouth. It came from deep down in her stomach, where some part of her had already taken in what her brain was still refusing to analyse.

They were going to take control over her. Again.

She felt as if she was being suffocated. It was a familiar, frightening sensation that came back from the past to take her over. A hostile spirit was emerging from a hiding-place where it had been waiting and watching. It was ready for her now. In spite of all her efforts, she had failed to exorcise it after all.

Anybody who fancied reading all about her in the paper could go right ahead. What had they all been saying back then? Silly-billy Sibylla. Something odd about that girl. Always reckoned she'd go downhill.

She clenched her fist in her pocket.

Was it her fault that she didn't fit in? She had never been one of them, but managed all the same. What more could they ask? She was a survivor, a survivor *in spite of everything*.

Now they would take her apart again, seeing her strength as madness and her unconditional existence as a loner's misery. They were poised to crush her plans to build a life of her own.

She wasn't going to let them, no way – not now.

'It wasn't me!'

She was phoning from a telephone booth in Stockholm Central Station. The line went silent, so she said it again.

'It wasn't me who killed him.'

'Killed whom?'

'Jörgen Grundberg.'

A brief pause.

'Who's that speaking, please?'

She was scanning the great station hall. It was a Saturday and the hall was full of people, leaving and arriving, ready to meet or to separate.

'I'm Sibylla. The person you're looking for. But I'm not the killer.'

A man carrying a briefcase was standing just a few metres away. He looked demonstratively first at his watch and then at her. Obviously, he was in a hurry and would like her to finish her call. Presumably he too had discovered that this was the only phone around that was still coin-operated. She turned her back on him.

'Where are you?'

64

'It doesn't matter. The important thing I want you to know is that it wasn't me who . . .'

She fell silent and looked out again. The man was still there, staring irritably at her. She turned her head away again and lowered her voice.

'. . . not me who did it. That's all I've got to say.'

'Wait a minute!'

She had intended to put the receiver down but stopped. She could sense the effort the woman at the other end was putting into formulating what she planned to say.

'How do I know that I'm actually speaking to Sibylla?'

'What's that you said?"

'Could you give me your ID number?'

Sibylla almost laughed. For Christ's sake, now what?

'My ID number?'

'Lots of people phoned today, saying that they're Sibylla. How do we know that you're the right one?'

She was open-mouthed with astonishment.

'Listen, I *am* Sibylla Forsenström. I've forgotten my ID number, I've had no reason to use it for a long time. I just wanted to say "Please mind your own business, leave me in peace".'

She had forgotten the waiting man, but when she turned he looked away, pretending not to watch her.

'Where are you?'

Sibylla snorted and stared into the receiver.

'None of your business, mate.' She finished the call and held out the receiver to the waiting man. He hung back, looking anxious.

'Come on, it's all yours.'

He gestured defensively.

'No, no, it's all right.'

'No? And you were so fucking keen a moment ago?'

His rolled-up evening paper stuck out from his coat pocket. It was *The Express*. She spotted one of her own eyes under that appalling fringe.

'Whatever.' She put the receiver back.

The man smiled nervously, then turned and left.

She had to get away now. Better being angry than scared. Above all, she mustn't ever stick her neck out. From now on she couldn't be sure who knew her by name and why. Christ, of all the names in the world, why did they have to pick *Sibylla*?

It had been easy to find out where Mrs Grundberg lived. The papers had printed so much information about Jörgen Grundberg that she could have written his biography.

The train journey to Eskilstuna didn't take long. She started off hiding in the toilet, but once the conductor had done his first ticket round and unlocked the toilet door from the outside, she went to find a seat. No one registered surprise at her sudden appearance in the compartment. Ever since discovering that one of the fittings on her hair-curling kit was ideal for opening locked toilet doors on trains, she had been treating herself to the odd excursion. She'd been caught just once and ordered off the train in Hallsberg, which wasn't too bad a place anyway.

She felt happier now, for some strange reason. Maybe it was because she was determined to take control over what was happening to her. Or maybe spending her last kronor on a hamburger had cheered her up.

The Grundbergs' large villa was surrounded by a chest-high wall of the same white, glazed bricks that covered the façade. Mock-Victorian lamps lit the driveway to the mahogany-style front door that contrasted with black-stained window frames. One of the largest satellite discs she'd ever seen was perched on the roof.

The whole place was screaming *more-money-than-taste*.

For a while she hung about on the pavement, hesitating. Then she walked round the block to avoid attracting attention by loitering and the walk helped her to make up her mind. She had better start trying to find an explanation here and now.

The decision was easy to reach in her head, especially on the far side of the block, but her legs were not keen on taking her along the drive. Looking at the large house, her courage was faltering again. The dark windows, framed in black and with black shutters, seemed to be observing her like so many hostile eyes.

Someone opened the door and called to her.

'Are you from a newspaper?'

'No.' Sibylla swallowed hard, closed the gate behind her and walked down the last part of the drive without looking at the woman in the doorway. Halfway to the front steps she passed a water-feature with a vaguely classical marble female, which presumably spurted water on good days. Now she looked frozen.

Sibylla stopped at the bottom of the steps, swallowing once more before looking up at the woman waiting there.

'Yes?' She seemed impatient.

'I'm sorry to disturb you, but I wanted to see Lena Grundberg.'

The woman shifted a little. She was in her forties and exceptionally good-looking.

'I am Lena Grundberg.'

Sibylla felt uncomfortable. She had no idea what or who she'd been expecting. Her idea had been to pretend she was a minister on call, or maybe a counsellor from some bereavement support group. The papers often mentioned that sort of thing. People, who simply came along uninvited, wanting to comfort the distressed widow or mother or whoever. Trouble was, this woman was looking just as cool and collected as the marble lady in the pond.

'What's the matter?' Her voice sounded a little cross, impatient. The tone was that of someone interrupted in the middle of watching an exciting film.

Having taken in the woman's personality, Sibylla made an instant decision to change her approach. Submission seemed the best way to deal with Lena Grundberg.

'My name is Berit Svensson. I know this is a terrible time to call but . . . I've come to ask you for help.' She blinked shyly. Looking up she saw Lena Grundberg frowning.

'I've been reading the papers, of course, and I live . . . round here. You see, I've lost my husband too, some six months ago and I still feel . . . I need to talk to someone who knows what it's like.'

Lena Grundberg, who was looking rather disapproving, seemed to be weighing the pros and cons. Sibylla decided to pile on the pressure.

'You must be such an incredibly strong human being. I'd really appreciate if I could just come in and talk to you for a moment.'

The last clause had the fervent ring of real truth and this small shift of nuance may have made the flattery convincing. Lena Grundberg stepped back from the threshold and gestured towards the hall behind her.

'Come in. We'll talk in the drawing room.'

Sibylla took one long step forward into the house. Bending down to take off her shoes, she realised that the large rug was very expensive. Next to her stood a wildly ornamental umbrella-stand in dark green metal.

The doorway between the hall and the drawing room had been remodelled into a wide arch. Lena Grundberg walked ahead of Sibylla, who kept looking around. Regretting the make-up she'd put on in the train, she wiped off the lipstick on her hand. Her instinct told her that the more superior the immaculately made-up Lena Grundberg felt, the better it would be.

Sibylla had extensive experience of that kind of woman.

The drawing room was so tasteless that she looked around in desperation for something to praise. She homed in on the one item that wasn't positively repulsive.

'What a lovely wood-burning stove!'

'Thank you. Do have a seat,' Lena Grundberg said and sat down on an armchair covered with leather in a shade like ox-blood.

Sibylla settled into the huge leather sofa. She was lost in amazement at the glass-topped table in front of the sofa. Its undercarriage was a naked marble woman, lying on her back and balancing the sheet of glass on her raised hands and knees.

'Jörgen imported marble,' Lena Grundberg explained, adding 'among other things.'

Jörgen was clearly part of the past already. Just like that. Lena Grundberg seemed to have read her thoughts.

'I suppose you'd better know from the start that my marriage wasn't especially happy. We were about to file for a divorce.'

Sibylla considered this.

'I'm so sorry.'

'It was my initiative.'

'Oh, right. I see.'

The room fell silent. Sibylla felt a little bemused. What had she imagined she'd gain by coming here? She couldn't even remember now.

'How long have you been a widow?'

The question was so sudden she jumped. Pointlessly, she looked at her watch. It had stopped again. She had to say something.

'Six months and four days.'

'What did he die from?'

'Cancer. It was very quick.'

Lena Grundberg nodded.

'Were you happy?'

Sibylla looked down at her nails. Thank goodness she hadn't painted them. She spoke very quietly.

'Yes, very.' Another moment of silence.

'It's so strange, you know,' Lena Grundberg said. 'Less than a year ago, Jörgen was dying from a serious kidney problem. He was hospitalised for months. Finally they decided that he could live normally again and all would be well for as long as he took his medicine in good order. On the whole, he was OK.'

She was shaking her head.

'And then he goes and gets himself murdered. After all that trouble. It may sound very cynical to say so, but frankly, it was absolutely typical of him.'

Sibylla found it hard to hide her surprise.

'How do you mean?'

Lena Grundberg lifted her eyebrows.

'He was such a lecherous fool. Taking an unknown female to your room like that, honestly – and so ugly too. One look at that photograph was enough to tell you she must be desperate.'

Stay cool now.

'You sound bitter.' Sibylla tried to keep her tone neutral.

'Not really. It's just that I think he could've picked someone better looking. I might have felt a little happier if . . .'

Her voice cracked suddenly. She was sobbing, hiding her face in her hands. How about that? At least one of the marble sisters was all emotion, once you got through the layers of foundation.

Considering Lena Grundberg's outburst, she almost regretted that Jörgen hadn't been allowed to share her bed. She should've let him, from pure human sympathy.

'You wanted him to choose someone who'd begin to match you?' Sibylla just about managed to control her voice, to keep the irritation out.

Lena Grundberg recognised the change of tone and tried to pull herself together. Her mouth still hanging open, she wiped the tears away carefully so as not to ruin her mascara.

'Yes, that's it, you know. It really would've helped.'

Sibylla was looking at the woman opposite her, reflecting that, after all, she'd never met anyone quite like her.

'Why would it have helped?' She was actually curious to know. 'After all, you were the one suing for divorce.'

Now Lena Grundberg was back in charge, leaning back calmly in her vulgar armchair.

'I do realise that it sounds selfish, but it's humiliating for a woman to be replaced by a complete nobody, an ugly whore picked up in a hotel. It's so . . . tasteless.'

Oh yeah? Hey, what about this room? The inside of my rucksack looks a whole lot better, so don't sit there and fucking preach about good taste! Sibylla swallowed twice.

'You can't be sure she was a whore, can you?'

Lena Grundberg snorted, bent down to pick up an evening paper from the floor and held it out for Sibylla to see. She glanced quickly at the photo of her own face. Surely only the nose was the same.

'How can the police be so sure she's the killer?'

Lena Grundberg dropped the paper on the floor.

'They'd gone to see the receptionist together about her room. By the morning, she was gone despite the police cordon. Seems pretty conclusive to me. Her fingerprints were all over the place. Like on Jörgen's room key.'

'What if it isn't her? Would you know if he'd had any . . .'

She stopped at the last moment and pretended to cough. She had been about to say '. . . any enemies in Lithuania or Latvia?'

She carried on coughing to cover her error. Lena Grundberg fetched a glass of water and Sibylla drank gratefully.

'Thank you,' she said. 'Sorry. I'm an asthmatic, you see.'

Lena Grundberg nodded and sat down again.

'Had no what?' she asked.

'What did you say?'

'You asked if I'd know if he had any – what?'

'Enemies, I guess . . . or something.'

Lena Grundberg was looking at her. Maybe

it was time to go. She was getting ready to stand when the woman opposite her suddenly uttered one word, filled with contempt.

'Sibylla!'

Sibylla started, as if slapped. Their eyes met. She stayed where she was, very still.

'It's such a weird name. No normal person is called Sibylla.'

Sibylla tried breathing calmly. It had been a scary moment.

'You're right, it's really peculiar.' She sounded ingratiating. 'Though presumably the woman didn't pick it herself.'

'Oh no?'

Lena Grundberg was not good company. Sibylla wanted to get away. Still, she had taken such a lot of trouble to get here, it would be silly not to try finding out something more.

'How did he die?'

The other woman coughed.

'She slit his throat first. Then she cut him open and spread out his organs all over the floor.'

She might have been describing a new recipe.

Sibylla felt she needed air. Now. Nausea came in waves. She rose.

'I've got to go.'

The widowed Mrs Grundberg stayed in her armchair.

'I suppose I didn't exactly meet your expectations?'

For once she could answer truthfully.

'No, not really.'

Lena Grundberg nodded, looking down.

'We all deal with things differently.'

Sibylla nodded too.

'Of course . . . thank you for letting me talk to you.'

She put her shoes on in the hall. Lena Grundberg remained sitting where she was and without another word being said, Sibylla quietly left the house.

Her walks were her salvation. 'Going out for a walk' was a legitimate reason to leave the house and the fresh air blew away some of her stale teenage angst. Her routes were always taking her to the edge of town, avoiding the hot-dog stall in the centre. It was *the* Hultaryd meeting-place for those who cared about meeting up. Sibylla wasn't one of them. It was a long time since she had positively wanted to meet anybody she knew from school in the evening. Seeing them there during the day was more than enough.

The Young People's Society for Motor Sports ran a community centre in the outskirts. It was a shabby two-storey house with its ground floor turned into a mechanics' workshop. The distance from central Hultaryd was a measure of the low status of the YPSMS members, but at least in some cases alienation seemed to be what was wanted.

She would probably never have noticed him, if she hadn't happened to pass just when he was bending over the engine of a souped-up old banger with very fancy paintwork. She stopped some twenty metres away to admire the effect. The car was pea-green with vivid flames streaming from below towards the rear wings. She had never seen anything like it.

She was trying to hang about casually, but after a while he looked up and spoke to her.

'Cool, isn't it?' He was wiping his oily hands on a rag.

She nodded.

'De Soto Firedome, from '59. I just had it back after a re-spray.'

She couldn't think of any response. There seemed to be nothing to say. Most of all, she was amazed that anyone in Hultaryd had been able to paint the flames so beautifully.

'Want a go? Just try sitting in it?' When she still didn't answer he shut the bonnet and waved at her. 'Come on, have a look. The seats are covered in real leather.'

She came closer. He was obviously keen to show off his car, which seemed innocent enough. She had never been in a car like that and couldn't remember ever having seen him before. He looked quite a bit older than her.

He threw the oily rag away. Then he wiped his hands on the sides of his jeans and opened the passenger door for her. After only a few seconds' hesitation she did what he obviously wanted her to do. The seat upholstery felt like an armchair.

'It's a great car. V-eight engine, 305 horse-power.'

'Great.' She smiled cautiously at him.

He went round to the driver's side and opened the door.

'Can you reach the blanket on the back seat?'

Sibylla got hold of the brown, checked blanket and handed it to him. He put it on the seat before he jumped in.

'Coming along for a drive?' He was already turning the key.

She stared at him.

'I'm not sure . . . I should go back home . . .'

The engine was humming. He pressed a button and her window went down.

'Electric circuit operating the windows. You want to check it out?'

She pressed the button. The window closed smoothly. She looked at him again, meeting his smiling face. Two dimples had appeared in his cheeks.

He got into gear and put his arm along the back of her seat. Her heart was beating harder now, because his gesture seemed so intimate even though it was probably just practical. Looking out through the rear window, he reversed into the road.

How come she was suddenly sitting in a suspect-looking car next to a complete stranger? What if anyone saw her?

'I'll drive you home. Where do you live?'

Sibylla swallowed.

'No, don't. Let's just go for a drive,' she replied quickly.

They drove towards the centre. Sibylla was watching him surreptitiously. There were spots of oil in his face.

'I'm Mick, but I won't shake hands. Unless you want to get oil on yours.'

'Sibylla.'

'Sure. Forsenström's daughter. That's right, isn't it?'

'Yes.'

He was driving down Tull Street and soon they would be passing the hot-dog stall.

'Hey, listen, isn't she sounding just great?'

Fantastic. Sibylla wasn't going to say the car sounded about as smooth as Gun-Britt's little Renault. The usual crowd had gathered around the hot-dog stall. Sibylla kept her head down.

'Those are your mates, right?'

At first she didn't answer and he looked quickly at her.

'Like, they're hanging out at your place.' He was grinning at his own joke.

She didn't even smile. Noticing her reaction, he too became serious.

'Come on, I was just kidding. Don't worry about it.'

She looked at him, realising that he really had meant it as a joke, not sarcasm aimed at her. The difference was obvious and she smiled back at him.

'No, they're not my mates.'

Not much more was said between them at that first meeting.

He took her back to the YPSMS place and she thanked him for the drive. He pulled the handle that released the bonnet just moments after she'd got out of the car. When she had walked away a bit, she turned. He already had his head down, tinkering with the engine.

A new, expectant feeling was growing inside her, making her certain that something important had happened, something good. Whatever it was, it mattered to her.

How right she was.

Of course, she couldn't have known that if the car hadn't been delivered that day, or if the paint had taken just an hour longer to dry so that Mick wouldn't have been outside working on it or if she'd taken her walk in another direction . . . or if, if, if . . . then, if things had happened differently, her life might have turned out quite differently.

That afternoon she had arrived at one of life's significant forks in the road, unremarkable-looking at the time, but where the effect of turning one way or the other is fully understood only afterwards. It would take her a long time before she realised it.

Then – much later on – it would become clear to her how wrong her choice of direction had been on that critical afternoon.

She walked away from the smart villa environment of the Grundbergs, following directions to the town centre. That night, she slept outside the door to the attics of an apartment block. The entrance door hadn't been locked. This vulnerability was one of the nice things about trips to the provinces. In Stockholm people were so careful that she usually had to stick to familiar addresses where she knew the score.

She was woken by some kid screaming further down the stairway, followed by the noise of a door opening and a woman's voice saying crossly that if he was going to be like that, he couldn't come along, so there. A little later the main door slammed and the place became silent again. She checked her watch, but it still didn't work. She really needed a new one, but watches were expensive.

When she got up from her camping mat, the world went black around her. She had to lean against the wall until the dizziness went away. Food – she needed food at once.

The station was only a few blocks away.

She went into the Ladies' Room to wash, comb her hair and put on mascara and lipstick. The green suit was creased from being in her rucksack, but never mind. Without it she'd go without breakfast. After putting it on, she held her hands under the tap and flattened the creases with her wet palms. It helped with the worst ones, anyway.

Putting the rucksack into Left Luggage meant that she'd have to pay to get it back later, but she'd fix it somehow. Food was top of the agenda now.

Surveying the scene from the station steps, she decided on the nearby City Hotel. She hurried across the street, then drifted into the foyer at a much slower pace. The male receptionist hurried towards her at once and she smiled at him.

'Goodness, it's so chilly today,' she said and shivered.

He smiled back. His golden name-tag told her that he was called Henrik.

'I just popped across to the station to check the train times, but I really needed a jacket.'

'Do ask us here in the reception next time, we've got all the timetables.'

She leaned confidingly towards him across the counter.

'Don't tell, but to be honest I took the chance to smoke a cigarette.'

He looked benignly at her, as if to reassure her that her secret was safe with him. The guest is always right.

So far, so good.

The hook for the key to room 213 was empty, but 214 was still in place. She looked at her watch.

'Please phone room 214 for me.'

'Of course.' He handed her the receiver. The signals rang out, but nobody answered. Henrik turned to check the keys.

'He should be in, his key is still here. Perhaps he's already gone down to breakfast?'

He nodded in the direction of a corridor.

'It's unlike him to be early, I must say. There's a first time for everything I suppose . . . But thanks. Have you got a morning paper I could have, please?'

He gave her a copy of *Dagens Nyheter* and she walked off towards the corridor, which would surely lead to the breakfast room. Easy-peasy.

Half an hour later she leaned back in the chair feeling full and relaxed. There were four other guests, all at separate tables and engrossed in their newspapers. Nothing new, it seemed, or at least *Dagens Nyheter* ran only a small column on an inside page referring to the police search for the woman who got away from the Grand Hotel.

The breakfast buffet was generous. She went up for a refill of coffee and managed to smuggle several breakfast rolls and three bananas into her handbag.

Back at her table, she thought about the excursion to Eskilstuna. Had she gained anything by coming all this way to let Jörgen Grundberg's widow insult her? She drank another mouthful of coffee, looking vacantly through the window.

Actually, she knew perfectly well what her trip had been in aid of. She had made herself believe that, equipped with some first-hand information and a contact with somebody who knew Jörgen Grundberg, she would be able to explain the whole story of their encounter in the hotel. The misunderstandings would be sorted out and the case closed, as far as she was concerned.

Instead, the outcome had been the opposite of what she had hoped. They were all utterly convinced that she had done it. No other candidates. What were her options now?

She could simply go into hiding. After keeping out of sight for the best part of fifteen years, it shouldn't be impossible. The published picture was the only one they had, which made her pretty unrecognisable now. As usual, her name spelt trouble and there were people who knew her usual hang-outs. Still, hardly any of them cared much for the police.

In other words, everything might sort itself

out if she lay low, avoiding a few obvious places until they caught the real murderer. Then she could live normally again. Goodness, never in her wildest fantasies had she thought 'back to normal' would be her aim in life.

After drinking some more coffee, she realised what was still disturbing her so much.

The humiliation. She had been so determined to take no more of it, ever. No more shit.

She had a clear vision of her mother's rage on hearing that her daughter had disgraced the family again. What's wrong with the girl? Being truly her own mother's daughter, the expression in her eyes would soon also say 'I told you so – don't say I didn't warn you.'

The gossip would be soaking through every layer of society in Hultaryd. You've heard about the Forsenströms' daughter, haven't you? She's a murderess.

Her father would probably . . . but no, she couldn't begin to imagine how he would react. She had never understood how he really felt about things.

By now she didn't care anyway.

She got up. Walking past the reception on her way out she waved to Henrik, who was on the phone, gesturing to show that she was slipping out for a smoke. He waved back.

Getting the rucksack out from Left Luggage turned out to be simplicity itself. There was no one about, so she walked unseen round the counter and lifted it off the shelf.

She changed back into jeans and sweater in the Ladies' Room. It was silly to use the green suit too often and besides it required dry-cleaning, which was an unforgivable luxury. The next train to Stockholm Central departed at 10.48, so she settled down on a bench to wait.

Coming home that afternoon, she sensed that something was wrong the moment she crossed the threshold. She called out but there was no response. In the drawing room she saw her mother sitting on the sofa, reading a book with her back turned to the doorway.

'Mummy, I'm home.'

Silence. Her heart was beating hard now. What had she done?

After hanging up her jacket, she slowly walked into the drawing room. Even though she couldn't see her mother's face, she knew what it would tell her. Her mother was upset. So upset and disappointed, darling. As she walked round the sofa, a lump was growing in Sibylla's stomach.

Beatrice Forsenström did not look up from her book. Sibylla forced herself to say something, but could scarcely find her voice.

'Mummy, what is it?' No sound came from her mother who carried on reading as if Sibylla did not exist, let alone had actually spoken to her.

'Why are you angry with me?'

Silence.

By now the lump in her stomach was so big it made her feel sick. Who had told her mother about this afternoon? Had someone seen her? She swallowed.

'What have I done?'

Still no reaction from Beatrice, who just turned a page in her book. Sibylla stared at the carpet. Its twisting oriental pattern began blurring in front of her eyes and she bent forward to make the tears fall straight down without leaving any traces on her cheeks.

Her ears were ringing. The shame of it all.

She went upstairs, knowing full well what to expect. Hours of anxious waiting for the explosion, hours more of guilt, shame, regret, longing to be forgiven. Please, please, dear God, let the time pass quickly. Please let her tell me soon what's up so I can say sorry – forgive me. But whatever You do, don't let her have found out everything.

God, don't take today away from me.

But sometimes God is hard. When the downstairs dinner-bell rang, Mrs Forsenström still had not deigned to appear in Sibylla's room. Sibylla was feeling really sick now and the smell of fried potatoes made her want to vomit. She knew what would come next. She would be made to beg and plead to be told what she had done wrong. Beatrice would speak only when sated with her daughter's self-abasement.

89

She arrived at Stockholm Central at 12.35. The Grand Hotel murder was definitely not in the news that day. The posters ran an animal welfare story, which had raised a storm of public indignation. After a few years in Sweden, a chimpanzee had been sold to a zoo in Thailand, where he had been confined in an unsuitable cage that was apparently far too small.

Leaving the station, she walked on past the Culture Centre at Sergel Square, where she usually spent many hours going through the newspapers in the reading room. She didn't feel like reading the papers. Never cared much for monkeys. She could do with a no-news day and above all no Grand Hotel murder stories.

Even so, she suddenly found herself sitting on a bench on the Ström Quay, her back to the water and her eyes fixed on the façade of the Grand Hotel just opposite. The cordons had gone. A limousine had drawn up in front of the main entrance and the chauffeur was chatting with the door porter. It was looking exactly as it had three days ago when she had innocently stepped inside.

'Hey, what's this? Sitting here contemplating your sins?'

She jumped, as if struck. It was just Heino, who had crept up behind her. He had brought all his worldly goods along, mostly plastic carrier bags full of empty cans. She knew that somewhere underneath the load was a rust-coloured hooded pram, because she had been around when he nicked it. Now only the wheels were showing.

'Christ, you really scared me!'

He grinned and sat down next to her. The odour of ingrained dirt immediately overwhelmed every other smell. She backed off as little as possible, in case he would notice.

Heino was looking at the Grand Hotel.

'Did you do it?'

Sibylla glanced at him, surprised at how fast the rumour had done the rounds. Heino wasn't the newspaper-reading type.

'No, I didn't.'

Heino nodded. He clearly felt that the subject had been exhausted.

'Got anything then?'

She shook her head.

'Nothing to drink. Fancy a fresh roll?'

He rubbed his filthy palms together, smiling happily.

91

'Now you're talking. A nice, fresh roll is a thing of beauty.'

She rooted around in her rucksack for her cache of breakfast rolls and gave him one. He ate greedily. The few teeth left in his mouth were struggling bravely with the roll.

'Great stuff. A chaser would be something else, though.'

She smiled, wishing she had any kind of drink for him. Preferably alcoholic.

Two smartly dressed ladies were approaching, leading a small dog kitted out in a tartan coat. It looked like a large pampered rat. Catching sight of Heino, one of them started whispering to her companion and both speeded up. Heino had been watching them and, just as they were passing, he rose and leaned towards them.

'Good afternoon, ladies. Would you be wanting a bite?'

He was holding his half-eaten roll in his hand, politely presenting it to them. They walked past without a word, obviously eager to get out of harm's way without humiliating themselves by breaking into a run.

Sibylla was smiling broadly as Heino settled back on the bench.

'Watch out,' he shouted after them. 'A rat's coming after you!'

The ladies walked very fast all the way to the main stairs of the National Museum, stopping only when they got there to check that no one was pursuing them. They were talking agitatedly. When a police car came driving across Skepp Bridge, the ladies' body language told Sibylla that they were going to hail the police. Her heart was beating faster.

'Listen, Heino, please do something for me.'

The police car had pulled in to the kerb now. The two women were talking and pointing towards their bench.

'If the pigs come here, you don't know me.'

Heino looked at her. The police car started up.

'Don't I know you? Sure I do. You're Sibylla, Queen of Småland.'

'Please, Heino. Not now. Please. You don't know me.'

The police car pulled in near their bench. Two uniformed police climbed out, a man and a woman. They left the engine running. Heino stared at them, stuffing the last piece of roll into his mouth.

'Hi, Heino. Did you annoy the ladies over there?'

Heino turned to look at the ladies. They were still standing at the entrance of the National Museum. Sibylla was peering into her rucksack, hoping to avoid police scrutiny.

'Me? No, I'm just quietly eating my roll.'

To prove his point he opened his mouth wide, displaying what was in it.

'Just as well. Keep eating, Heino.'

Heino shut his mouth, muttering crossly to himself.

'Easy for you to say.'

Then he carried on chewing. Sibylla was taking an intelligent interest in a side-pocket on her rucksack.

'Now, has he been bothering you at all?'

Sibylla realised the policeman was talking to her. She looked up, rubbing her eyes as if a piece of grit was troubling her.

'Who, me? No, not at all.'

She opened another side-pocket and started rummaging again.

'I'd never bother queens. Specially not the Queen of Småland,' Heino said earnestly.

Sibylla closed her eyes, but kept fiddling with the rucksack. One more side-pocket to investigate.

'I like that, Heino. That's the ticket.'

The woman constable was trying to round off their chat. To her relief, Sibylla could hear them both walk away and open the car door. Glancing at them, she saw the male PC still holding the door handle.

'What's your problem? Why are you spying on honest citizens peacefully eating their stuff? So the old hags are out walking their rat and start making a fuss, taking offence at nothing whatever – is that my fault?'

'Shut up,' Sibylla hissed.

Heino was becoming heated. The police stopped in their tracks.

'Let me tell you something you don't know, right? Like, you might just have been of some use if you'd turned up here on the twenty-third of September, in the year of eighteen hundred and eighty-five.'

The policeman was approaching now, but the woman stayed in the passenger seat of the car. Sibylla began closing the various compartments of her rucksack. Time to beat it.

Heino rose, pointing towards the Grand Hotel.

'That's where she was standing, on the Grand's balcony.'

Sibylla stopped to listen.

'Down here it was packed with people, all the way across to the Kung Garden. They were waiting for her to sing.'

Now Sibylla and the policeman were both staring at him. The policeman was curious.

'Who was singing from the balcony?'

Heino sighed and shrugged, spreading his dirty palms.

'Don't you know anything? Christina Nilsson, that's who. The Nightingale from Småland.'

Heino stopped dramatically. The policewoman began to get impatient. She lowered the car window to shout at her colleague.

'Janne, come on!'

'Hang on a minute.'

Heino nodded, totally in control.

'More than forty thousand were crammed into central Stockholm, wanting to hear her sing. This place was black with people. Folks were clambering up lamp-posts, standing on top of carriages, wherever. In dead silence. Do you know, her singing was heard all the way to Skepp Bridge. Get it? Those days, people knew how to keep their mouths shut.'

'Janne! I'm waiting!'

Heino had caught the policeman's attention completely. All Sibylla could do was sit tight, letting it happen. She glanced towards the National Museum. Heino lifted his arm and raised a finger in the air. The movement sent another wave of foul smell wafting from his worn coat. Sibylla concentrated on holding her breath.

'The moment she'd finished singing they all started applauding like lunatics. Then somebody shouted that the scaffolding around the Palmgren Mansion was coming down. They were building there at the time. First the crowd got worried, then it panicked. Sixteen females and two little kids died after being trampled underfoot. Another hundred or so were taken to hospital.'

Heino nodded again.

'You lot should've been around then, they might have lived longer if you had. Doing your policing thing properly, instead of getting at me. I'm just eating my roll.'

The policeman called Janne was beaming at him.

'Right you are. Interesting story, Heino. Take care now.'

This time he managed to get into the car and drive away before Heino thought of something else to say. Sibylla kept staring at him, shaking her head.

'How did you know all that?'

Heino snorted.

'Education. Have you heard of it? I may smell like shit, but I've got an education.'

He rose, swinging his loaded pram round in readiness for raiding the Kung Garden rubbish-bins.

'Thanks for the roll.'

Sibylla smiled wanly and Heino left while she was still looking at the balcony where Christina Nilsson had been standing, one hundred and fifteen years ago. Nowadays there wasn't a hope of hearing someone sing above the incessant roar of the traffic. Turning her head, she was just in time to see Heino disappear after crossing Kung Garden Street. She felt a fleeting impulse to run after him. It would be good not to be alone, just for a while longer. But it was no use.

She stayed where she was. The hullabaloo about the murder was not yet past its peak. Better keep herself to herself.

As usual.

After that first trip in his car she stopped by the YPSMS house to see Mick practically every afternoon, their times together growing steadily longer. In the end she jettisoned the idea of going for a walk and simply went straight there. She met the other YPSMS members, who were all guys, the same age as Mick, same style. For the first time she felt accepted into a group. Because she was with Mick she was OK, no further qualifications needed. They even seemed indifferent to the fact that she was Forsenström's daughter.

Still, being alone with him in the workshop was the nicest thing about coming there, mainly because Mick seemed much more relaxed when it was just the two of them. He happily taught her all he knew about engines and cars. Sometimes he would take her for a drive and, when he was in a really good mood, leave her at the wheel on quiet forest roads. The first time, he told her to sit in his lap while she practised the controls. She felt his thighs under her own and his stomach against her bottom.

Her whole body seemed to respond strangely to these contacts. She felt hot and tense. Then she became very aware of his hands over hers on the steering wheel.

When she came home after that trip she wrote his name under the seat of the chair in her room. He was her secret. This secret seemed to confer a miraculous strength on her, which must have showed somehow. Maybe because she didn't bother listening any more, the name-calling in school troubled her less and her daily routine became more bearable.

The whole day would pass in the expectation of seeing him again. She wanted to smell him, stand next to him as he was bending over the innards of the car to show her something. She was full of admiration for his grasp of every detail and loved seeing his hands move knowingly among the parts of the engine.

She longed to be in the same room. With him, close to him.

After the summer holidays she began upper school and had to travel to Vetlanda. Her own choice would have been the course in Mechanical Engineering, but she had enough sense not to mention this to anyone but Mick. Dropping even the tiniest hint to her mother would have been rash. Mrs Forsenström felt that the three-year Economics course was suitable for preparing Sibylla to pull her weight in the family firm. Also, it was an option with a bit of class.

Of course, she did exactly what her mother wanted.

On days when Mick had an errand into town, he picked her up after school. She hid until she missed the school bus. A couple of blocks away from school the De Soto would be waiting for her, a sight that always filled her with eagerness and pride. Blissfully leaning back into the seat, she would be driven the forty kilometres back to Hultaryd.

Never to her home, not even within sight of it.

Once during one of these school runs, he turned off the main road and drove along a forest track not far from Vetlanda. She looked at him, but he kept his eyes on the road. Neither of them spoke.

Inside, she knew what would happen. She had been expecting it. He stopped the car, they got out and then stood there facing each other for a moment.

She came towards him full of trust, feeling that she belonged to him. She was his chosen one.

He had spread out the brown checked blanket for them to lie on. Gently, he pushed into her.

She was his alone. And he was hers.

She was watching his face out of the corner of her eye, amazed at the pleasure she was able to give him. He was absorbed in her. His whole mind was focused on her, his body intent on hers. He gave himself to her.

Two of them, locked together. She would do everything for just seconds of such closeness. Anything.

The fried potatoes were expanding into an unmanageable lump in her mouth. Her parents were chewing in silence.

It was pure anguish, waiting for the eruption of anger.

She couldn't swallow.

There were two forks in her hand. No, three. The table was moving up and down. She had to swallow. But the fear in her stomach wanted to come back up.

Swallow. For God's sake, swallow. Don't make it any worse than it is.

Forgive me. Please forgive me. Tell me what I must do to be forgiven. Don't keep me waiting, please.

I'll do anything to be forgiven.

Anything at all.

Beatrice Forsenström put down her knife and fork. She still avoided looking at Sibylla as she opened the abyss with a simple statement.

'Sibylla, I understand you're riding about in somebody's dreadful old car.'

A woman with a bulldog saved her. Sibylla spotted the woman from a distance, standing on the corner of Gräs Street where the path to the Eriksdal allotments began, alone but gesticulating energetically. As she came closer, she spotted the small loudspeaker ear-piece and the flex connecting it to the mobile phone. It was the latest mobile gadget, meant to keep precious parts of the brain from being microwaved to a frazzle, or so the papers said.

'It makes me so effing furious! If you pardon my French.'

Curiosity made Sibylla slow down almost to a standstill. The bulldog had settled down at the feet of his agitated mistress, looking at her with real interest.

'Christ almighty, is this some police state we're living in or what?! So you're looking for some freak on the run? Frankly, I don't give a monkey's. When I'm out walking in Sweden I don't expect to have a gun shoved into my face all of a sudden. It's bloody well out of order.'

By now Sibylla was rooted to the ground.

'Calm down? Don't hold your breath! I'm not feeling calm at all! I'm going to charge these gun-toting lads of yours, take my word for it. Made me show my ID card before letting me walk my dog . . . I ask you! Not a word of apology did I get either. I'll get somebody for this!'

The woman fell silent for a while, listening to someone on the other end of line. She glanced at Sibylla, who promptly looked the other way.

'I see . . . yes. No, I won't. And if you don't accept my complaint I'll take it elsewhere.'

The woman pocketed her mobile. Her dog got up.

'Kajsa, come on!'

The woman and her dog crossed the street. Sibylla still did not move.

'Don't go in there.'

Sibylla smiled at the woman.

'Why not?'

'It's crawling with police in there, but out of sight. You don't know they're there until you get a gun shoved in your face. No idea what they're up to. Made me furious, I can tell you.'

Sibylla nodded.

'Sure, thanks. I think I'd rather avoid all that.'

The woman and her dog wandered off, leaving Sibylla breathing deeply. It must have been Uno Hjelm. The allotments' own little old Judas. Fuck him.

She had to get away. Fast.

*   *   *

How long could she stand living like this? Surviving, that's one thing. She could do that. She had done it. But being on the run . . . ?

She was hurrying now, feeling that they were already at her heels. God, how could Hjelm have spotted her? Surely he couldn't have recognised her from the photo in the newspapers? If so, she was lost, unsafe anywhere.

She had to change her hair. She was close to Ringen now. There were plenty of people about and she could just mingle with the crowds. But weren't people staring at her? How odd it was. What about the man walking towards her, why did he look at her like that? Her heart was beating hard. She looked down and the man walked past her.

If she told them the truth, would they believe her? Couldn't they understand that she had simply wanted to sleep in a proper bed, just for once? She would have paid him later. Of course she would have! She had . . . lost her wallet. Really.

Lots of people were converging on the underground station. She kept walking.

But – where was she going?

Once on Renstierna Street she changed direction and walked up the steps leading to the Vitaberg Park with Sofia Church towering above her like a fortress. She was tired and needed to sit down for a while. Turning, she checked the deserted path sloping down towards the street. No one had followed her.

The silence inside the church seemed solid, tangible. Just inside the door was a glass-fronted cubby-hole. An elderly man peered at her through the glass and nodded. He seemed friendly. She nodded too, before taking her rucksack off and stepping inside.

The church was empty apart from someone sleeping in one of the pews, a man with his hair in a pony-tail. The pony-tail guy was vaguely familiar, she'd seen him a couple of times at the City Mission Centre. Now he was in a deep sleep, his jaw drooping toward his chest. She sat down in a pew at the back with her rucksack at her feet. Closed her eyes.

Peace and quiet, simply. It was all she wanted.

The man in the cubby-hole coughed. The sound reverberated between the walls. Then the silence solidified again.

God hears your prayers. It said so on a poster near the door.

She opened her eyes again and spent some time examining the huge altarpiece. Over very many years, very many people had put their lives in His hands. They built enormous edifices for the worship of their God and turned to Him in their prayers. When she was little, she too prayed to Him. 'If I should die before I wake, I pray to God my soul to take.' Then: 'Dear

God, look after mummy and daddy and make it so they don't die.' He must have heard that bit, since they were apparently getting on very nicely, thank you. 'When I lie down and go to asleep, I pray the Lord my soul to keep.' Keeping my soul seems to have slipped His mind. Maybe He is wholly on their side?

Well, on all their sides, the sides of those who fit in.

Where did the stationmaster's prayers end up? He jumped off Väst Bridge last month, after realising that his fourth detox treatment had failed. Was anyone up there listening to Lena? She used to be on the Salvation Army's food vans, but she had to stop because she had an inoperable brain tumour. Exactly what had Lena done to deserve that? What about Tova? Or Jönsson? Or Smirre? All dead, after subsisting for years in his or her own special living hell. Presumably none of their prayers were ever heard.

God, this prayer story of Yours simply doesn't wash.

Come to think of it, what about Jörgen Grundberg? Whatever he might have been punished for, why bring me into it? Am I supposed to be punished for something? And if so, *when* will my punishment be over and done with?

She sighed, rose and heaved the rucksack onto her back. There was no peace to be found here. She left the church without looking at the man in the cubby-hole.

The sun was setting when she came out of the church. She stepped back to see the church clock. Quarter past five.

She would really have liked to sleep in a bed tonight, but hotels were too risky and she didn't even dare try the Klara doss house. They were always short of room, so if she got a bed, then someone who hadn't and was in the police's bad books, might well do a little informing to make up for past sins.

She felt for the purse round her neck. She was tempted to draw on her treasure, for the first time since she made up her mind about saving. A real drinking session, so she could forget for just one night.

Shit. What rotten stinking luck.

She turned into the lane leading to Skåne Street. About twenty metres along was a charming small piece of cultural history, a green door set in a wooden fence painted a nice shade of red. To the right of the door the fence joined the gable-end of a humble wooden house. She stopped and examined the wall of the house. The hatch of what might have been the coal-chute was almost level with the ground and had been nailed into place. A second opening about a metre up had a door with only a peg through a hook to hold it shut.

She looked around. The park was empty.

In a moment she had taken off her rucksack, opened the little door and climbed inside.

*T*hursdays were our days, the days when he came to me. If I close my eyes, I can see him open the garden gate down by the road and start walking along the gravel path towards me. I remember how I felt warmth from my heart spreading through my whole body. He always took such care wiping his shoes on the doormat. There he was, wrapping me in his strong arms. Dear Lord, this was love and not sin. Love, such as You have taught us it should be. I thank You for letting me experience it.

Every time he came I had prepared the house as nicely as anyone could wish. I wanted him to realise how much I had been looking forward to seeing him. Every time I hoped he would not leave. But staying was impossible and he always left at four o'clock in the afternoon. When that hour struck I knew I had another seven days of waiting ahead and seven endless nights, full of longing to see him again. Now my whole life is such a night.

Yet I thank You, God. I am grateful for your guidance. You have shown me what I can do

*to help him enter Your realm, so that I can rest
assured that he will be there for me when my
time comes. Thank You God for letting me be
your ally in the sacred work of correcting the
errors of the unjust on Earth.*

*Lo! I tell you a mystery. We shall not all sleep,
but we shall all be changed in a moment, in the
twinkling of an eye, at the last trumpet. For
the trumpet will sound, the dead will be raised
imperishable, and we shall be changed. For this
perishable nature must put on the imperishable
and this mortal nature must put on immortality.
When the perishable puts on the imperishable
and the mortal puts on immortality, then shall
come to pass the saying that is written:*
    'Death is swallowed up in victory.'
    'Oh Death, where is thy victory?'
    'Oh Death, where is thy sting?'
    *The sting of death is sin and the power of sin
is the law. But thanks be to God, who gives us
victory through our Lord Jesus Christ.*

*God, I too wish to thank You for Your protec-
tion. You have not left me alone in my task but
sent that woman to shelter me. You are allowing
her to atone for her sins by giving her a sacred
purpose. For this I thank You, Lord God.*
    Amen.

She had no idea where she was when she woke. She recognised the sensation, but this morning it seemed especially hard to make sense of her whereabouts. The light was seeping through the cracks in the wooden walls, falling on the rubbish that surrounded her. She remembered where she was only when the bells of Sofia Church rang out seven times.

She sat up to eat her last banana.

The floor was broken and covered in sawdust. Last night she had put planks across the joists to arrange somewhere to roll out her mat. She ate slowly, watching the dust whirl in the beams of sunlight.

Her sore throat wasn't troubling her any more. She definitely needed a shower after tonight. Central Station was no good, because the police were always about. She didn't dare go to the Klara shelter either.

Keeping track of time had become problematic since she'd left her diary in the Grand Hotel, but she was pretty sure her charity hand-out should be there today. First of all she just must do something about her hair. If she borrowed some money from her savings to buy hair dye, she could collect the money afterwards.

Having extracted a twenty-kronor note from her savings, she caught the 76 bus to Ropsten. Normally she avoided buses, because it was easier to get through the underground check-ins without paying. This was the first time in six years that she had used saved money. Fourteen kronor for just one journey, what a waste!

Fucking bastards, all of them.

At first, she was the only one at the Renstierna Street bus stop. When people started turning up, she looked away. It was the morning rush-hour, but luckily she found two seats right at the back, one for her and one for her rucksack. When they reached Slussen all the seats had been taken and a woman standing close by her was eyeing the rucksack. Usually it wouldn't have bothered her, but just now she didn't want anyone watching her. She hauled the rucksack into her lap and the woman sat down, taking a morning paper out of her briefcase.

Sibylla kept looking steadfastly through the window as the bus crossed Skepp Bridge and pulled up at the traffic lights. It was next to a newsagent and the shopkeeper was putting up fresh news posters. When the bus started, he had moved enough for her to see the text. Automatically, her eyes recorded it and sent it straight to her brain.

It couldn't be true!

She sat staring blankly ahead for what seemed like an age, confusion and fear pumping through her body. A noose was tightening round her neck.

A passenger's face turned her way. Instinctively she pulled at the rucksack to make it into a bigger barrier and by shifting her position saw what her neighbour was reading. She didn't want to, but once more her eyes were recording things against her will.

The headline alone made her feel sick.

She didn't want to know any more and she forced her eyes to focus on the rucksack for the rest of the journey, not daring to move until the woman got off at her stop.

The paper was left on the seat. She didn't want to. Knew she had to. Fuck them.

She grabbed the paper before getting off the bus.

On her way to Nimrod Street, she popped into the Co-op and bought a packet of Rich Black dye, raiding her savings for the second time that morning. She would pay every single kronor back the moment she got her hand-out envelope from the post office box.

The Nimrod Street block of flats was an invaluable asset to her and a few others in the same predicament. Everyone in the know was exceptionally tight-lipped about it. It was information she had paid dearly for. Not in money, though.

The main door was always open and because the flats lacked showers, a couple of well-equipped shower-rooms had been built in the basement. The rooms were spacious and smartly tiled, had a lavatory with plenty of toilet paper and unlimited quantities of hot water.

They were locked, of course. Only the initiated knew where to find the spare key, fastened to a large piece of wood, in its hiding-place inside an old iron wall-cupboard just next to the doors leading to the wonderful washing facilities. Even better, you could lock the shower-rooms from the inside.

That key was worth more than its weight in gold.

As soon as she got in, she put her panties in the basin to soak, using a few drops of shampoo instead of washing liquid. Next, the hot shower. She was in luck, someone had left a bottle of conditioner. She closed her eyes, but the headline seemed fixed in her mind's eye.

Was there no end to this? Would she ever wake from this nightmare?

THE GRAND HOTEL MURDERESS STRIKES AGAIN

NEW RITUAL MURDER IN VÄSTERVIK

'For how long have you been carrying on like this?'

It was her father speaking, for once. Sibylla swallowed again. The tabletop still seemed to rise and fall in front of her.

'Like what, Daddy?'

Her mother snorted angrily.

'Sibylla, don't pretend. You're not such a fool you don't understand what upsets us.'

True, she did know. Obviously she had been seen in Mick's car.

'We met in the spring.'

Her parents looked at each other across the table, behaving as if they were joined by elastic bands.

'What is the man called?'

'Mikael. Mikael Persson.'

'And do we know his parents?'

'I don't think so, they live in Värnamo.'

No one spoke for a while and Sibylla found some respite in the silence.

'How does he earn his living in Hultaryd?

I assume he's in employment.'

'He's an engineer. Car mechanic. He knows everything about cars.'

'Is that so?'

They looked at each other again, more closely bound to each other now. The rubber-band ties that connected them were tightening and loosening, but their faces were blank, empty. Sibylla looked away.

'We do not approve of our daughter being seen in one of those disreputable cars.'

She thought, it's not disreputable, it's a '59 De Soto Firedome.

'In fact, you must not socialise with that kind of person, with none of these boys.'

Her head felt like a lump of lead. It tipped over towards one side, too heavy to be straightened up again.

'They're my mates.'

'Sit up straight when we're talking to you!'

Her head shot upwards automatically but her neck could not keep it upright. Instead it tipped backwards, hitting the top of her high-backed chair.

'Now, what's the matter? Sibylla, what's wrong with you?'

Her mother had got up and was advancing. Sibylla's head was stuck to the chair at first, but then it slid sideways and followed her body to the floor.

*   *   *

'Sibylla, how are you?' It was her mother's voice.

She was lying somewhere soft and there was a cold, damp thing on her forehead. She opened her eyes and realised she was in her own bed, with her mother perched on its edge and her father standing in the middle of the room.

'Dear child, you really scared us.'

'I'm sorry. Forgive me.'

'Now, now. We'll talk about it later.'

Henry Forsenström came closer.

'How do you feel now? Shouldn't I call Dr Wallgren?'

Sibylla shook her head. Her father nodded to show that he had registered her answer and left the room. Sibylla looked at her mother.

'I meant that I'm so sorry I fainted like that.'

Beatrice removed the wet handkerchief that had cooled her forehead.

'You can't help fainting, Sibylla. No need to apologise for that. But about the other thing we were talking about, you must do as you're told. Your father and I agree, you must never go to that place again.'

Sibylla was close to tears.

'Please, Mummy.'

'Your weeping and wailing is simply pointless. We're just thinking of what's best for you, you know that.'

'But the people there are my only friends.'

Her mother pulled herself up straight. She was losing her patience. As far as she was concerned, the discussion was finished.

Yes, it was finished, like everything else.

A long, relaxing shower was usually a sure-fire way to cheer her up, but it didn't work this time. If anything she felt even more miserable when she was drying herself afterwards, as if hope had gone down the drain with the water.

She took her wet towel and washed panties through to the laundry room on the other side of the corridor. The key worked its magic and she started the tumble-drier.

Back in the shower room, she locked herself in again to get on with her new hairdo. First she cut her shoulder-length hair. It fell in large strands to the floor. Doing the back was difficult and the more she trimmed away, the clearer it became that in future her chances of flirting her way to free nights in hotels would be minimal. Still, that option had been pretty effectively taken from her anyway.

Following the instructions carefully, she dyed the remaining tufts black. She ended up looking like an aged punk rocker. Not even fucking Uno Hjelm would recognise her now.

She tidied up meticulously, honouring the understanding among the initiated in the secret 'clean-living' society. The slightest trace of any outsiders coming and going might make the regular tenants hide the key in a new place.

When everything was in order, she settled down on the lavatory seat to wait for her things to dry. The newspaper was lying just inside the door. She hadn't found the courage to read it yet, but knew she mustn't put it off any longer. Taking a deep breath, she grabbed it.

Pages 6, 7, 8 and the centrefold.

32-year-old Sibylla Forsenström, charged in her absence with the murder of 51-year-old Jörgen Grundberg in the Grand Hotel, yesterday carried out another brutal murder. At about 3 p.m. on Sunday, a 63-year-old man was found murdered in his summer cottage just north of Västervik. The woman seems to have struck when the man was asleep and temporarily on his own in the cottage. The general method employed was identical to the murder of the Grand Hotel, but at present the police refuse to comment further on how the man was killed. They do, however, speak of both deaths as 'executions'. Both victims were grossly mutilated and had organs removed from the body. The police have not given any further details. Allegedly, the woman is suspected of being guilty of desecration as well as murder. The police statement emphasises that there is no discernible motive and that the victims seem to be picked at random.

Sibylla couldn't bear reading any more of this and turned the page. The first thing she saw was a drawing of a face alarmingly like her own. The waiter in the Grand Hotel dining room must have an excellent memory for faces or maybe it was Hjelm, who had seen her with her hair down. Not that it would do much for him now.

Oh, God – she was so fucking deep in all this shit. What had she done to deserve it?

The police still have no definitive clues as to the whereabouts of 32-year-old Sibylla Forsenström and are looking for assistance from the so-called 'underworld' in Stockholm. Various informants claim to have seen the woman, for instance in Central Station, and in an allotment area on Södermalm. A national search warrant has gone out after the murder in Västervik. According to an unconfirmed report the woman had left a message with religious overtones, also admitting guilt, near the scene of the murder. So far there is no hint of a motive for either crime.

She got up hurriedly and vomited into the basin.

The entire Swedish police force was out chasing her now, because she was known to be an insane ritual killer. How could one bottle of fucking hair dye help? Her body was still convulsing, but having got rid of the banana her stomach had nothing more to offer. She drank some water and tried to calm down.

Someone was knocking on the door.

'Hi, will you be finished in there soon?'

She glanced at her face in the mirror. The jet-black tufts on her head were standing straight up and her face was ashen. The overall effect was of a fading junkie.

'I'm in the shower.'

Closing her eyes, she prayed to God that whoever it was would go away. Of course, He had no special reason to listen this time either.

'Please hurry up. The other shower room is occupied.'

'OK.'

Silence.

She opened her make-up bag, rouged her cheeks and put on lipstick. It didn't improve matters much, but at least it was obvious that she had made an effort. Then she wiped away the half-digested banana with toilet paper and cleaned the basin.

Listening at the door, she heard nothing except the noise of the tumble-drier. She had no choice but to tough it out. It would just seem even more suspicious if she crept out looking ashamed. She stepped outside briskly.

He was sitting on the floor outside, reading a book.

'That was quick. I didn't mean to hassle you.'

When she came out, he rose. Then he saw her rucksack and looked bewildered.

Sibylla pointed to it and smiled.

'It's for the laundry.'

He nodded.

When she tried to open the door to the laundry room, her hand shook so much it was almost impossible to insert the key with its foot-long board into the keyhole. Finally, the door clicked open.

'Have you just moved in?'

She avoided having to look at him by walking up to the tumble-drier.

'Yes, that's right.'

'Cool. Hope you like it here.'

She thought, if you don't bugger off to your shower I'll kick you where it hurts.

She took out her panties and towel, quickly pushing the still damp washing into her rucksack and watching from the corner of her eye as he went inside the shower room. Just as she was getting out of there he came back out, holding the newspaper in his left hand.

She stiffened suddenly and came to a halt, as if her feet had stuck to the concrete floor.

For a moment he looked confused again, then he held the paper out towards her.

'Don't look so worried, it's just that you forgot your paper.'

The annual Christmas Party, once more. She was seventeen, sitting at the high table.

She'd asked her mother to be let off but received mock surprise for an answer.

'Why, darling? You'd enjoy an evening out, surely? You've been sitting at home for months.'

Too true. Certainly, she'd been sitting at home. It had been sixty-three days and nine hours since she last saw Mick. Every day Gun-Britt had collected her from Vetlanda in the tiny Renault. The afternoon walks had been forbidden, on the grounds that trust had been abused.

'I don't want to go.'

Her mother didn't answer. She just went into the dressing-room to find a suitable frock for her daughter's evening out.

'Don't be silly, darling. Of course you'll join us.'

Sibylla was sitting on her bed, watching her mother pick and choose in the wardrobe.

'I'll come if I'm allowed to sit with the other young people.'

Beatrice was stunned by this unheard-of ultimatum.

'Now, what's the reason for this, may I ask?'

'They're my age, that's why.'

Her mother turned round with an odd expression on her face. Subjected to her mother's gaze, Sibylla's heart started pounding. She had made up her mind, telling herself that she wasn't alone any more and could always run to Mick. In seven months' time, she would be eighteen years old and free to do what she liked. Until then she was going to fight for every inch. Her voice was quite steady.

'If I can't sit with the others I'll just stay here.'

Her mother could not believe her ears. This was, of course, an incredible statement. It worried Sibylla that she couldn't interpret the look on her mother's face. A sense of unease began tingling under her skin. She felt just the tiniest whiff of fear.

'You know perfectly well that this is the most important evening of the year for your father and me. Now you want to ruin it. Don't you ever consider anyone except yourself?'

The pendulum was swinging her mother's way. Beatrice was ready to trigger a major explosion and there was no doubt at all about who would suffer the consequences. Suddenly, real fear gripped her. It must have shown, because her mother changed her tone.

'There now, we'll talk about this when we get back home.'

Beatrice sailed out of the room, having suc-cessfully crushed her daughter's will.

The Sales Manager sat to her left. Mr Forsen-ström, the CE, was enthroned in the central seat.

Sitting at the high table in her party frock, Sibylla felt strange. The whole room was hum-ming, somehow. The noise from the hall came in waves and even her neighbours' talk reached her only intermittently. She had not touched her food yet, but the others had finished. Her mother was smiling and proposing toasts round the table, but every time her eyes met Sibylla's the corners of her mouth turned downwards, as if pulled by gravity. The anger radiating from Beatrice was transmitted in Sibylla's direction in such forceful pulses that she thought the glasses in the way might shatter.

But it was exactly at this moment, as Sibylla was waiting for whatever elaborate punishment was in store for her, that she felt strongly that enough was enough. Her anger welled up with unexpected violence. That woman had turned her existence into a never-ending imprisonment. In Sibylla's eyes her mother was transformed into an absurd monster.

Yes, she had been born out of that body. So what? It hadn't been her choice. It was a

126

mystery why God should have allowed this woman to bear a child at all. All her mother had wanted was living proof of the Forsenström family's general excellence. A child confirmed that everything proceeded according to plan.

In fact, nothing worked properly. Sibylla suddenly saw how much her mother enjoyed every step in the obedience-chastisement-punishment routine that had become established in their home. Beatrice manipulated her daughter's fear, relishing her ownership of the child.

'How are you getting on at school then, Sibylla?'

The Sales Manager was asking his annual question. He was about as interested in her answer as in some muck on his shoe.

'So kind of you to ask,' she said loudly. 'Mostly we just hang out, boozing and fucking.'

He nodded benignly. A second later, his tiny mind registered her answer and he looked the other way, plainly at a loss. The high table guests stopped speaking as if on pain of death. Her father was looking straight at her, his expression more confused than upset. Maybe he wasn't quite sure what 'fucking' meant. Her mother's facial colour shifted towards purple.

The whole social carousel was spinning wildly around her, but Sibylla felt calm and in control. The Sales Manager's glass of brandy was standing within easy reach and she lifted it in a toast to her mother.

'Cheers, Mummy. I just thought of something. Why don't you get up on a chair and sing a Christmas song for everyone? It would be so nice.'

She emptied the glass. By now the entire room had fallen silent. She took the opportunity to stand up and address them all.

'Hey, what do you think? Wouldn't it be great if dear Beatrice here sang a little song for us? Full of Christmas joy!'

Every single eye in the room was riveted on her.

'You don't want to? Why, don't be shy, darling Mummy. You mustn't worry. Why not simply go for that rather foul little ditty you hum in the kitchen most nights?'

Finally, her father broke free from his state of paralysis and spoke, his powerful voice echoing through the room.

'Girl, SIT DOWN!'

She turned to him.

'You talking to me, Daddy? For you are my Dad, aren't you? I remember seeing you around at home, like at suppertime. How are you? My name is Sibylla.'

He was staring at her, slack-jawed.

'This is getting really boring. I think I'll be off. Have a lovely evening, everyone!'

Seventy-six pairs of eyes followed her as she walked through the silent room, all the way from the podium past the tables to the door that led to freedom. When she closed the door behind her, she breathed in deeply and felt truly fresh air filling her lungs for the first time in her life.

S he dumped the newspaper in a rubbish bin in Ropsten tube station. The ticket had been paid for properly with another twenty-kroner note from her treasure trove. She dared not cheat in case she ended up drawing attention to herself. Standing on the platform waiting for the Lidingö train, she thought grimly that Stockholm Transport had now got more money off her in one day than it had over the last fifteen years.

It was half past twelve and there were relatively few people in the train. She examined her image in the window-pane. How weird she looked! This would surely give her a little more time. Maybe she would be able to work out how to deal with it all. First, she must collect the money from her post box and return the money she had spent to her savings. They mustn't be allowed to take her hope away.

Her post box.

Oh fuck.

The insight sent a high-voltage current through her body. How could she have been so bloody stupid that she hadn't figured the police would've got her number by now?

She was just wandering blithely into a trap. It was highly likely that the police knew of the one fixed point in her existence. Her name was attached to that post box. Of course they would have discovered the only register that had her name in it.

Once she saw the full extent of her loss, rage started boiling inside her. So, she'd never be able to collect her money again? She was unconsciously balling her fists, feeling her anguish fade and being replaced by defiance. They were not going to do this to her. If she'd been a respectable person, sticking to the social norms, they would never have treated her like this. She had never demanded anything from society and she didn't intend to start now.

She could take so much shit being poured over her but no more. Now she would fight.

Thomas lived in a boat, anchored at the Mälar docks on Långholm Island. She got off at Hornstull and crossed the Pålsund Bridge.

Thomas was the only person she trusted enough to ask for help. Ten years ago, before he inherited the houseboat, they'd been living together in a caravan parked in the Lugnet industrial area. Now and then the police would knock on the door with a warrant to move them on and each time they pulled the caravan a few metres away, settling down again to wait for the next attempt to shift them.

On the whole, they'd been left in peace. There was no question of being in love with each other, but they both needed human warmth and company. That was all they had to offer each other and at the time it had been enough.

She had not been there for many years and at first she couldn't see his boat. Walking back along the quay, she finally discovered it next to a camouflage-painted Navy vessel. Mooring space must be hard to come by.

Taking her rucksack off and propping it up on a pile of wooden pallets to keep it out of the wet, she suddenly had last-minute doubts about Thomas. When he got drunk, he ceased to be a trusted friend. She still carried several scars which proved the point. She breathed in deeply, clenching her fists to rekindle the fighting spirit.

She looked around, but the quayside was deserted.

'Thomas!'

'Thomas, it's me – Sylla!'

A head popped up above the railing on the Navy boat. He had grown a beard and was barely recognisable. His expression was baffled at first, but then his face broke into a large grin.

'Christ, it's you! Haven't they got you locked up yet?'

She had to smile back at him.

'Are you alone?'

'Sure thing.'

She knew him well enough to know he was sober.

'Can I come in?'

He didn't answer at once, just kept looking at her and smiling.

'Would I be safe then?'

'Come off it! You know I didn't do it.'

The smile widened.

'No problem then. Open-door policy. Just leave all sharp objects behind on deck.'

The face vanished again. Thomas was a real friend, maybe her only one. Just now this mattered more than anything else.

He had left the hatch open and she lowered her rucksack down to him, then started down the ladder. The space that was once the hold was serving both as a home and a joinery workshop, possibly never cleaned this century. Everything was covered in sawdust and pieces of sawed wood, confirming that he wasn't living with anyone now. Good.

He followed her eyes which examined the room.

'I guess it looks the way it did last time you were here.'

'No way, it was really neat and tidy then.'

He smiled and went to start the coffee-maker. What might be loosely called the kitchen corner contained a table, three odd chairs, a fridge and a microwave oven. No empty bottles in sight, which was another good sign.

'Fancy a cuppa?'

She nodded, watching as he emptied the old coffee into the wastepaper basket. The inside of the coffee-maker jug was coated with a black film. Settling down on the soundest-looking chair, she watched Thomas filling the jug from a large plastic bottle.

'So what sort of shit are you in?'

She sighed.

'You tell me. I wish I knew.'

He turned to look at her.

'Why the hair?'

She didn't answer. He pointed to *Aftonbladet*, sticking up from the rubbish bin.

'The hairdo in that picture was nicer.'

Then he emptied the old contents of the filter into the bin, absentmindedly slopping some of the grounds on the floor.

'You probably won't want to know, but I wondered if you'd help me with something.'

'What's that, then? Me giving you an alibi?'

Suddenly she felt irritated at him, even though it was obvious that he kept joking just because he was nervous. She recognised it, but this time the humour was lost on her.

'Come off it, I was in the Grand. It's the truth. But you know perfectly well why it's a little hard for me to explain to the police what I was doing there.'

He sat down opposite her.

The coffee-maker started spluttering behind him, the first drops landing somewhere inside the blackened jug. He must have picked up the new note in her voice, because he suddenly became serious.

'Chasing a night on the house, was that it?'

She nodded. He pointed at the paper in the bin.

'And that's the guy who paid, every which way?'

She nodded again.

'Christ. That's rotten luck. What's that Västervik story about?'

She leant back, closing her eyes.

'Not a clue. I haven't set foot in Västervik in my whole life. I'm lost, honestly.'

She met his eyes. He was shaking his head.

'Fucking bad break.'

'You can say that again.'

He started scratching his beard, still shaking his head slowly.

'Sure, I see – so, what do you need help with?'

'Getting my mother's money. I don't dare go anywhere near my post box.'

They eyed each other across the table. 'Sylla's mum's dosh' was a familiar concept to them both. During their years together in the caravan, he had helped her spend it on booze. He rose to get the coffee, picking up a mug in the passing.

The handle was broken and it obviously hadn't been washed since the first time it was used.

'You eaten today?'

'No.'

'There's cheese and bread in the fridge. Help yourself.'

She got up, even though she didn't feel hungry any more. Still, it would be silly to miss out on a chance to eat. When she came back with the loaf and the chunk of cheese, he had poured the mug full of coffee for her. He was scratching his beard again.

'Thomas, you know I wouldn't ask if I didn't have to. I'd go under without the money.'

'OK, I'll see what I can do. So . . . I'll go there and try. For old times' sake.'

Their eyes met again. For as long as he stayed sober his friendship was invaluable to her. He was her only secure contact with the outside world. But if he started drinking he would demand a pay-back.

For old times' sake.

As soon as she left the party, she started walking to the YPSMS house. No one tried to stop her. Presumably her mother was working hard to save what was left of the party mood at the annual Christmas do.

The night was cold and she had forgotten to bring a jacket, but nothing mattered now. Light fluffy snowflakes were floating down from the sky like glittering confetti. She tipped her head back to catch them in her mouth. She felt brilliant.

Her life had been freed of fear, nothing worried her any more. She was fine, on her way to Mick. The world was her oyster.

People dressed in white were lining the road, waving at her and calling her name jubilantly, like in the film she had seen on TV last Saturday. Light followed her as she walked, as if a spotlight was moving with her every step. She waved back to the delighted people and swirled around among the snowflakes.

The De Soto was parked outside the workshop. The thought that Mick might not be there simply hadn't occurred to her. She was in control. Of course he had to be there.

She bowed to her audience, still standing in the road looking after her. Then she opened the door and stepped inside, taking a deep breath to fill her lungs with that longed-for smell of motor oil. She felt joy bubbling inside her.

'Mick!'

Something moved behind the stack of tyres at the back of the room. The spotlight was still following her as she walked across to see what it was. Before she got there, Mick's head rose from behind the tyres.

'Hi Sibylla. What are you doing here?'

Some half-conscious part of her brain registered that he didn't sound pleased, in fact almost irritated. She smiled at him.

'I've come back to you.'

He was looking down at something out of sight as if he was buttoning his fly . . . or something. But it couldn't be that.

'Sibylla, this isn't a good time. Why don't you come back tomorrow?'

Tomorrow?

What was going on? She walked closer, saw the brown checked blanket spread out behind the tyre-stacks. On it lay Maria Johansson.

The spotlight was switched of. Darkness surrounded her.

But she had been chosen to be his, only his.

His body had joined hers in ecstasy, wanting her only. Two of them linked together.

Together.

Anything for this closeness. Anything at all.

She looked at him. His face seemed to have gone blank. She backed away from him.

'Sibylla . . .'

Her back hit the opposite wall. The door was to her right. Push the door handle down.

The happy crowd was no longer there for her but the De Soto Firedome was waiting with 305 horsepower under its bonnet.

A few steps, open the door. Key in the ignition.

She wanted to be away. Far away.

She had been alone in the boat waiting for almost two hours when he came back. Walking up and down like a haunted spirit, her mind had been lurching between hope and despair, anguish and conviction. What if they were keeping watch at the post boxes? What if Thomas wasn't on his guard? What if they followed him and he led them straight to her only safe hiding-place?

Come on. Look, Thomas has been around. He'd be careful, no question about it.

Why was he taking so long? Had they arrested him?

His footfalls on the tin roof of the cabin alarmed her terribly, even though she had been longing with every cell in her body to hear them. Then the hatch was pulled open.

She hid behind the mounted chainsaw, shut her eyes and waited. Like a cornered rat.

To hell with them all.

He was alone. After climbing down the ladder he stood still, looking around.

'Sylla?'

She came forward.

'What took you so long?'

He went over to the coffee-maker and switched off the heater. More grounds got thrown in the direction of the bin.

'I wanted to make sure no one was trailing me.'

'Did anyone try?'

'No, don't think so. All peaceful on that front.'

In a mute question he pushed the coffee-jug in her direction. She shook her head. He breathed in deeply, so deeply it sounded worryingly like a sigh.

'Listen, Sylla. There wasn't any money.'

She was staring at him while he put the jug back.

'What do you mean?'

He gestured, striking out with one arm.

'Your post box was empty.'

He had to be lying.

For fifteen years now, on the twenty-third of every month, an envelope containing 1,500 kronor had arrived in her post box. Every single month. She pulled the paper out the waste-paper basket, spilling coffee grounds all over the floor. The date-line said Monday, 24 March. She looked up, facing him.

'You . . . Christ. I trusted you, Thomas.'

He met her eyes.

'Is that fucking so?'

His eyes tore into her in a way she remembered from his fits of drunken rage, but she couldn't stop and feel frightened of him now.

'It's mine! I can't live without that money!'

He froze for a moment. Then he threw the mug, still half-full of coffee, into the far wall. Some tools on hooks crashed to the floor. The coffee flowed down the wall, forming a brown pattern. The crash made her stiffen but she didn't take her eyes off him.

He inhaled deeply as if trying to calm down and then went to stand at one of the portholes, staring at the nothingness outside.

'I admit I've done bad stuff. But you mustn't accuse me of nicking your dosh. You're just on the wrong fucking track there.'

He turned towards her.

'Didn't it ever occur to you that it'd turn the old hag off – like, why would she put her hard-earned cash the way of a manic serial-killer?'

His words took some time to sink in, slowly passing via her eardrums into her skull before she realised how right he was. This was the end of charity. Beatrice reckoned she had paid enough, settled her debt.

Sibylla's mind went blank.

She slowly went to the table, pulled out one of the chairs and sat down. Then she put her face in her hands and started to cry.

Now she was really lost. All her hopes had turned to ashes.

She wasn't meant to get through, to succeed. Once more, Fate had intervened to kick her down. Once a loser, always a loser. She had been challenging the established, set-order of the universe, trying to haul herself up to a place above her station.

Now, now, little Miss Sibylla Wilhelmina Beatrice Forsenström. You had your life nicely staked out for you, but did you appreciate it? You did not. You need never have gone hungry if only you hadn't decided to up and leave your proper place in the system.

Here today, gone tomorrow. Forever.

'Sibylla, don't cry like that.'

She felt his hand on her shoulder.

'Stay cool, Sylla, please. It'll sort itself out, you'll see.'

She thought, sure it'll sort itself out – I'll just have to serve life in prison first and after that I guess nothing matters much.

'I know what you need. To get pissed.'

Yes, that's right. Be unconscious, just for a while. Sozzled. That's what she wanted. He had already produced a full bottle of Koskenkorva vodka from a cupboard. She looked at the bottle, then at him. His face looked kind. She nodded.

'You're dead right. Let's drink.'

She had almost reached Vetlanda when the police stopped her. A red light was blinking at her from the middle of the road. She pulled over, two policemen materialised outside her window and she opened it. One of them leant inside, stopped the engine and pulled the key out. He withdrew, glancing to check her face.

'Now then . . . what have you been up to?'

She didn't feel scared. She felt nothing at all.

'Step outside for a moment, please.'

He opened the door and she stepped out. A car was pulling up behind the De Soto and Mick jumped out, running towards her. Maria Johansson stayed where she was, in the passenger seat.

'You fucking slut! I'll kill you if you've buggered up my car.'

One of the policemen put a hand on Mick's shoulder, telling him to calm down. Mick pulled himself free and climbed into the De Soto. The policeman handed him the keys. After checking what he could, Mick got out, turning to look at her with intense disgust.

'You're one insane cunt.'

She noted that the policemen were leading her over to their car, pushing her into the back seat with a hand on her head. One of them sat next to her and the other drove the car. Neither said a word to her from then on.

'Is your name Sibylla Forsenström?'

What was the funny smell in the room?

'Why did you take the car?'

What if it was gas?

'Have you got a driving licence?'

How come there were cracks in that wall?

'Can't you speak?'

The man on the other side of the desk sighed and began leafing through some papers. Four men dressed in black stepped through the cracked wall. They fixed their eyes on her.

'We can't find you anywhere in our records. Is it the first time you've done this sort of thing?'

The men in black were coming towards her. One of them held out a red-hot socket-spanner. They were going to unscrew her, take her apart.

'We shall have to contact the social services in due course, but first of all we'll call your parents. They can come and take you home now.'

They were going to keep bits of her as spare parts to fix smarter models. The man with the socket-spanner seemed to speak, his lips were moving but she couldn't hear what he said.

She looked at the man behind the desk instead, but his face had sort of disappeared. There was nothing there, just a hole going straight through his head.

Now she couldn't see anything at all, and what was she doing on the floor?

She heard the sound of a chair being pushed back and a voice shouting.

'Lasse, come here! I need a hand!'

Steps came hurrying along.

'I've no idea what's wrong with her. Better get the ambulance.'

She came to because someone was kicking her in the ribs, not violently but hard enough to wake her. Thomas was standing next to her, wearing nothing except a pair of underpants. She took in the scene in one second flat. He was drunk and he was holding a wad of notes in his hand, approximately twenty-nine thousand kronor.

Instinctively she put her hand to her neck, but where the money should have been was only her skin. In fact, she was naked. He was grinning menacingly at her, waving the purse in his other hand.

'You'd be looking for this, right?'

Her mouth felt like a sandpit. It was years since she'd drunk hard liquor. She couldn't actually remember drinking a lot, but the bottle on the table was empty.

'You cunt! Sending me off to the post office to get you more dosh! And snivelling because you can't manage, dear oh dear!'

She tried to think. Meanwhile she was too slow reaching out for her bra. A flick with his foot and it flew across the room. She covered herself with the flap of the sleeping-bag.

'Please listen, Thomas . . .'

He twisted his face into a grimace and spoke in a piping voice.

'Please, Thomas.'

His eyes had narrowed into slits.

'What got into you, fucking around with me like that? I was running a bloody big risk, the police could've got me for aiding-and-abetting or some shit. Meanwhile you've a sodding fortune up your jumper!'

He was scrunching the notes in his hand.

'I've been saving that for years.'

'Oh yeah. And?'

She was almost whispering now.

'For a house.'

At first he just stared at her, then leaned back, laughing. The movement almost unbalanced him and he had to reach out for the ladder. This sudden weakness angered him even more.

Before he had time to speak, she folded back the sleeping bag flap. Then she spoke as sweetly as she knew how.

'Thomas. Let's not fight. I was going to show you the money anyway.'

He was still holding onto the ladder. She felt nauseous.

'Thomas, I came here because I've been missing you.'

His eyes were glued to her breasts. She felt his

gaze touching her like hands and she had to steel herself not to shudder. He dropped her purse on the floor. She tried to keep smiling. Next he scattered her hopes for the future with one careless movement, the notes floating slowly towards the filthy floor.

The next second he had come down on her. She prayed that he would be quick.

*L*ord, give me strength to survive from hour to hour, from one day to the next. Help me face these empty days, the remainder of the vacant time left to me here.

He will be waiting for me somewhere in the great beyond. I shall go to him, find my treasure again. My heart will always be with him.

Truly, truly I say to you, he who hears my word and believes Him who has sent me, has eternal life; he does not come into judgement, but has passed from death to life.

Do not marvel at this; for the hour is coming when all who are in the graves will hear His voice and come forth, those who have done good, to the resurrection of life, and those who have done evil, to the resurrection of judgement.

I can do nothing on my own authority; as I hear, I judge; and my judgement is just, because I seek not my will, but only the will of He who has sent me.

God failed to hear her yet again. Thomas was taking his time. Finally, he had had enough and fell asleep on top of her like a suffocatingly heavy quilt. With infinite care, she managed to ease herself out from under him and stand up.

Still naked, she picked up her scrunched-up notes from the floor. She tried to flatten them against her thigh before putting them back into the purse again.

Thomas was sleeping on his side with his mouth open. A string of saliva was dribbling from his mouth into his bushy beard and soaking into the mattress. She was grateful that she hadn't used her own roll-up mat, because she would have had to leave it. Her sleeping bag had slipped off them and she retrieved it easily after lifting one of his legs.

She dressed quickly, longing for a shower to wash off the trail left by his eyes crawling over her body. It was unbearable – she must find a tap with running water to wash under. Packing her things, she noticed that her towel and panties smelled sour after being packed while damp. They needed another wash.

Where? Where could she go?

She wanted to get out and away as soon as possible, but was thirsty enough to risk staying a little longer. She drank from the plastic bottle and then let the water run over her face and hands to wash them. The sawdust on the floor was turning into a sodden slurry, brown with coffee grounds.

Thomas shifted the leg she had been pulling at and she stood stock-still until she was certain he was deeply asleep. She must hurry up the ladder and out into . . . into what, exactly? Not 'freedom', that was not an option any more.

Fuck them all.

It was dark outside. Old reflexes made her look at her unhelpful watch.

All the lanes of the South Mälarstrand carriage-way were empty and the windows in the big blocks of flats were almost all dark. Maybe it was still too early for people to be up and about.

Good. The less she was seen, the better.

She tiptoed across the deck and climbed onto the Navy vessel. Once back on the quay, she started walking towards the bridge. Her legs seemed to have a will of their own. Her head was empty. She had no idea where she should be going.

Still, that was quite normal.

In her world, not knowing where you were heading was the rule, not the exception. She sometimes asked herself if her block against planning ahead was connected to the illness of her youth. Perhaps it had damaged some part of her nervous system which was meant to deal with foresight. In her new life, finding something to eat every day and a sheltered place for her sleeping bag every night were the only things that demanded any thought at all.

Fair enough, you could live without any expectations higher than holding onto the freedom to move. This freedom was the basis for the way she lived. No one could tell her what to do. Her will was her only directive and she went only where she wanted to go.

Now all that had changed. She no longer knew where she wanted to go, not even where she could safely go.

She was walking along Heleneborg Street and then, where the rows of houses ended, turned into Skinnarvik Park. The sky was growing lighter. A man seemed to combine admiring the view with watching his dog defecate. Man and dog both looked up when they heard her steps on the gravel path. Then the man dutifully bent down to pick up the turd in a plastic bag, peering over his shoulder at her, as if she might object.

She walked on. There was a newly delivered

box of bread outside a restaurant at the corner of Horn Street. They surely wouldn't miss one of the loaves.

What she needed now was somewhere safe to shelter for a couple of days. A place where she would be left in peace, where no one would think of looking for her. Fear of pursuit had become her constant companion and it was exhausting. She needed rest. From experience she knew that without proper sleep her brain functioned less and less well. She would become easy prey if she lost her sense of judgement.

In her mind she was going over all the places she had ever slept in. Few had been as safe and quiet as the hide-out she had to find now.

By now there were more cars around. To avoid meeting the morning rush-hour traffic she decided to walk up Horn Street Rise. Passing St Mary's Church, she looked at the clock.

At exactly that moment she realised where she could hide.

D ays and nights, flowing into each other. The same faceless people speaking to her in alien tongues, oblivious of the dangers threatening her.

The ones without faces were wandering in and out of her room, holding out tiny cups with poison-tablets that they made her swallow. Meanwhile, voices were addressing her from inside the radiator and the Devil was hiding under her bed, waiting for her to get up. If her feet so much as touched the floor he would grab her, dragging her down into the big hole down there. Underneath, in the cellar, his black men would be waiting to work her over with their burning hot instruments.

She didn't want to sleep, didn't dare to. The pills they gave her made her lose consciousness all the same. When she was asleep there was no telling what they did to her. That was the reason they put her to sleep.

One unending nightmare.

When she refused to get up they stuck a tube

into her down there. They wanted to pump in more poison that way too. The stuff was yellow and they kept it in a plastic bag next to her bed. Then the Devil could top it up whenever he wanted to. When she tore the tube out, they tied her hands.

There was a man dressed in white who came to make her talk. He pretended to be kind but was only after her secrets. He would pass on what she told him to the men in the cellar.

Darkness and light following each other. Time ceased to be. New hands made her swallow the white poison-pills.

Then, one day, she suddenly understood what they were saying to her. They sounded kind, concerned to make her feel comfortable. They were protective and listened to her. One of them wheeled her bed across the room to let her see that there was no hole underneath it. Afterwards she agreed to be taken to the toilet and they removed the tube from her private parts and the yellow poison-bag from beside her bed.

The next day, everyone who came to see her had a face and smiled. They fixed her bed, plumping her pillows and chatting to her all the time. They still wanted her to take poison, though. She was ill and in hospital, they told her. She had to stay until she got better.

Then where would she go? She tried not to think of the 'afterwards'.

More days and nights passed. The voices from the radiator stopped speaking so much and finally left her in peace.

Sometimes she would go outside her room. There was a TV set at one end of the corridor. None of the other patients spoke to her, because they were all enclosed in their own worlds. Often she simply stood at the window in her room, leaning her forehead against the cold bars and observing the traffic outside. Everyone was getting on with life without her.

They took her for walks in the hospital park sometimes, but never let her out alone. The winter snow was melting by then and there were snowdrops growing in the borders.

Beatrice Forsenström came to visit her. The man who wanted to make Sibylla talk came as well. Beatrice was immaculately groomed, but there were dark shadows under her eyes. She kept her handbag in her lap when she and the man settled down next to the bed.

The man looked nice. He smiled at her.

'How are you feeling now?'

Sibylla was watching her mother.

'I'm much better, thank you.'

The man seemed pleased.

'Do you know why you're here?'

Sibylla swallowed.

'Maybe because I did something silly?'

The man was looking at her mother, who had lifted her hand to her mouth. Sibylla had made the wrong answer and her mother would be sad. No, disappointed.

'Don't worry, Sibylla. You've been ill. That's why you're here,' the man said.

She kept looking at her hands. No one said anything for a while. Then the man rose and spoke to her mother.

'I'll leave you two alone now, but not for long.'

They were on their own in the room. Sibylla was still looking at her hands.

'Please forgive me.'

Her mother suddenly got up.

'Stop that at once.'

Oh no, she had made Mummy angry as well.

'You have been ill, Sibylla. There's no need to apologise for that.'

Then she sat down again. For a brief moment their eyes met, but this time her mother looked away first. Not soon enough. Sibylla had a perfectly clear idea of what was going on behind those eyes. Beatrice was furious at her daughter for putting her in this situation, which was beyond her control.

Sibylla went back to studying her hands. There was a knock on the door. The man who wanted her to speak came back in, carrying a brown folder. He came to the end of her bed and spoke to her.

'Sibylla, there's one special thing both your mother and I want to talk to you about.'

He glanced at Beatrice, but her eyes were fixed on the floor and she was clutching her handbag so hard her knuckles were going white.

'Sibylla, do you have a boyfriend?'

She stared blankly at him.

'Do you have a boyfriend? I have a reason for asking.'

She shook her head. He came to sit next to her on the edge of the bed.

'This illness you've been suffering from, it can have physical causes, you see.'

Is that so?

'We've tested some samples we've taken from you.'

Yes, I know.

'The results show that you're pregnant.'

The last word went on echoing though her head. She had a vision of the brown checked blanket.

She alone would be his. Only his. And he hers. Together.

Anything for just a second of such closeness. Anything at all.

*   *   *

She glanced at her mother. Beatrice must have known all along.

The man who wanted her to speak put his hand on hers. His touch triggered a pulse of emotion that flowed through her body.

'Do you know who the father of the baby is?'

The two of them, together. Linked forever.

Sibylla shook her head. Her mother kept looking towards the door, her whole being longing to open it and get out of there.

'Your pregnancy is already in its twenty-seventh week, so a termination is not really an option for you.'

Sibylla put her hands on her stomach. The man who wanted her to speak smiled at her, but somehow didn't look happy.

'How do you feel?'

How did she feel?

'Your mother and I have been discussing this.'

Somebody started screaming in the room next door.

'Because you've not yet come of age and your parents know you better than anybody else, their views are taken very seriously. As your doctor, I fully support their decision.'

She stared at him. What decision? They couldn't do things to her body, could they?

'We all agree that adoption would be the best thing for your baby.'

She rarely granted herself the luxury of shopping in a 7-Eleven store, where the prices were always way above average. This time though, her usual rules had to go overboard. She needed enough food to keep going for a few days and she needed to buy it early, before the doors opened to Sofia High School. The idea was to get in as soon as possible, before the corridors filled with pupils and their observant teachers.

Minutes after seven o'clock, she had stocked up on baked beans, bananas, yoghurt and crisp-bread. She was ready to go, the moment the school porter or whoever unlocked the doors to paradise. She would be left in peace there.

By twenty past the school's 'responsible person', whoever he was, had done his duty. When he was gone, she crossed the street, went in through the main door and simply walked up all the stairs to the corridor at the top of the building, meeting no one on the way. It was an old building and her footfalls echoed between its stone walls. Up there, the door to the attic was just as she remembered it.

STAFF ONLY
NO ACCESS

Underneath the sign, the responsible person had placed a handwritten note, warning that the floor was in bad repair and in danger of collapse.

It couldn't be better.

The door was locked by an ordinary padlock. She sighed, missing her Victorinox pen-knife. Presumably it was part of the evidence in the case and stored in a police station somewhere. The loop in the wall was held by four screws. She rooted around in her rucksack for some kind of implement and found her nail-file. It had to work.

It did, in fact she had barely prodded at the upper screw before it came out. She felt a small, chilly shiver of suspicion. Did somebody else know about the quiet seclusion of this attic? Still, she had no time to reconsider. The rumble of voices from the floors below was growing and she went in, closing the door behind her.

Down a few steps. There was a handrail to hold on to. It was looking different now. She had been there six, seven years ago and since then the school had been renovated, that had been obvious from just walking up the stairs.

Last time, the attic had been full of rubbish and old junk, but the dodgy floor presumably meant that they had cleared away as much as possible. All that was left were a few piles of old textbooks.

She recalled that it had been summer back then and the heat under the poorly insulated roof had been suffocating. Maybe that was why the attic space was unused. Anyway, this time heat would not be a problem – on the contrary.

The clock was still where she remembered it. Seen close-up, the Sofia School clock was enormous. They had rigged up two lamps to light the clock-face. The clock had been broken then, but now she could see the minute hand moving. This worried her a little. How often did they need to fix the clock?

She forced herself to stop worrying. If she just kept her things along the far wall, she would have time to hide if some busybody suddenly turned up.

It didn't take long to roll out her mat and put the sleeping bag on top. She hung her panties and towel to dry on an electric cable. Tonight she had to find the staff-room shower and wash her smalls again, because if left to go sour they'd smell bad forever. She still felt dirty. Thomas's hands were far away by now, but somehow they had left her coated in a sticky film. Had he woken up yet and found that she'd gone? What would he do then?

So, here she was. Hidden in an attic. Humiliated, hounded and abandoned.

Over the years, she'd had so many reasons for giving in but something inside her had made her fight on. Maybe the moment had come, for was all this not reason enough? It might be a relief to finally admit that she was nothing but a mistake, from beginning to end.

She listened out for the noise of the pupils filling the school.

Silly-billy Sibylla. Sibylla's a banger, grill her. Sylla Bylla, kill 'er.

Maybe they had been right? They had found her out, smelled her otherness when she was just a child. All the time, people had just been following their instincts about her, sensing that she wasn't meant to join their groups. She hadn't understood at first and had to learn the hard way. Her stubborn fighting back had gained her a little extra time, which had not been hers by right. She and Heino, and all the rest of the outcasts, were a kind of undergrowth in society. They seemed destined to make the standard citizen feel more satisfied with his existence, by giving him a chance to rank his success relative to their failure.

Well, there are worse fates than always pitching your demands in life as low as possible, in the name of social balance. Sheep and goats are sorted from the outset, anyway.

She lay down. The bell rang and the whole building fell silent.

It would be so easy to give up. Accept that you were a lost soul, fit for nothing. She would never go to the police willingly, never ever, but there were other ways of giving in.

If she didn't have the strength to walk as far as Väst Bridge, something could surely be managed right here in the attic.

They had let her go home two weeks later. The silence in the large house was as solid as concrete. Gun-Britt had been given notice, presumably because Beatrice couldn't bear the shame of a servant observing her daughter's growing belly. As few eyes as possible must see it. Walks were strictly forbidden. After dark, Sibylla was allowed to wander in the garden, but never to stray to the wrong side of the fence.

Her father spent almost all his time at home in his study. Now and then she heard him walk across the tiled floor at the bottom of the stairs.

She ate in her room, her own choice after the first evening meal back home. It had been painful, her parents silent to the point of muteness but somehow still speaking volumes. How could she blame them? Her whole being was in contradiction to their expectations of a daughter. They had looked forward to showing off a model young person, proudly confirming the success and dignity of the Forsenström family. Instead all she gave them was the shame of a total failure, which must be hidden away from the prying, malicious eyes of the local citizenry.

No problem, she really preferred eating on her own.

She did not think often about Mick. He was a dream she had dreamt. He was somebody she met long ago. Someone who didn't exist any more.

Nothing that had been before stayed the same. Everything was different now.

She had been mentally ill.

She had become a person who had been sick in the head – gone mad, weird. Nothing could change that. What she had experienced she would never be able to share with anyone. No one would understand what it had been like. No one would want to try.

At the same time, a sense of having been unjustly treated was lurking inside her. It grew stronger day by day until it almost consumed her. It was unfair that she should be here, because she didn't want to stay. If she could, she would have left long ago.

She was carrying a load of guilt on her shoulders, made heavier each day as their disappointed eyes followed her around the house. All she wanted was to get away from them, but instead she was their prisoner. While she was waiting, her stomach was growing steadily bigger. What was she waiting for? What was it?

She was like a tool without a will of its own, helping to build the dream of two unknown adoptive parents-to-be. Her body was working for them.

Of course, everyone was becoming very keen on looking after her. Even her mother tried her best. Her swelling stomach became something she could hide behind now, but what would happen when it had gone?

Then what would they do about her?

The word 'adoption' had seemed purely descriptive, free of values. It just sounded like any ordinary word – 'percentage', say, or 'democracy'. It meant giving her child away.

She had to give away this thing that had turned up inside her body without being asked and made her grow bigger and bigger. Now she could feel it kicking when she was lying still. It was kicking against the tense skin on her stomach, as if wanting her to know it was there.

There was a knock on the door. Sibylla checked the time. It must be her supper.

'Come in.'

Her mother entered, carrying a tray, which she put down on her desk. Sibylla realised at once that there was something on her mind. Usually the tray ritual was quick, but now Beatrice was taking her time, apparently engrossed in arranging the place-setting just so.

Sibylla had been lying on her bed reading. She sat up, watching her mother's back.

'The vegetables, Sibylla. You didn't eat them yesterday. You should be eating lots of greens, it's important just now.'

'Tell me why.'

Her mother stopped in the middle of a movement. A few seconds passed before she answered.

'It's important for . . .'

She cleared her throat.

'. . . the child.'

Is that so? The child, now. It had taken time for her to get the words across her lips. The strain had been obvious, just by watching her back. Suddenly, Sibylla lost her temper.

'Why is it so important to look after the baby?'

Her mother turned slowly to face her.

'I haven't been getting . . . pregnant. It's up to you to take responsibility for your actions.'

Sibylla didn't answer, mostly because there was so much to say.

Her mother seemed to be pulling herself together. Obviously it wasn't just the vegetables she had wanted to talk about. The value of eating your greens had just been an unfortunate sideline. Sibylla watched her as she steeled herself to carry out her real errand.

'I want you to tell me about your child's father. Who is he?'

Sibylla did not answer.

'Was it the youth with the car? That Mikael Persson? Was it?'

'Might have been. Why? What does it matter?'

She could not stop herself. Her mother was trying hard to control her anger, but Sibylla wasn't going to help her. Not any more.

'I just wanted to let you know that he's not in Hultaryd any more. All the motor sports people had to go. Your father owned that property and he decided it was convenient to have it knocked down. I gather that Mikael has moved out of town.'

Sibylla had to smile. It was not the prospect of the YPSMS building being demolished that made her grimly amused, but the likelihood that her mother was not quite normal, mentally. It was the first time she was able to contemplate the possibility. Mum really seemed to believe that she was almighty.

'I thought you'd better know.'

Beatrice obviously felt everything necessary had been said and was about to leave the room. Her daughter's question hit her halfway across the floor.

'Why did you have a baby?'

Beatrice Forsenström's left foot stuck in the rug. She turned. Sibylla saw something new in her mother's eyes. She had never noticed it before, but now it was unmistakable.

It was fear. Beatrice was afraid of her own daughter.

'Was it because Granny thought it was time for you to produce a child?'

Her mother remained speechless.

'Are you happy to be a mother? At having a daughter?'

They kept staring at each other. Sibylla felt the baby stirring a little inside her.

'What did Granny make of me having a mental illness? Or haven't you told her?'

Suddenly her mother's lower lip started trembling.

'Why do you do this to me?'

Sibylla snorted.

'Why do I do this to *you*? You've got to be fucking insane.'

The swearword tipped Beatrice back into normal mode.

'We don't use words like that in this house.'

'Is that so? You don't, maybe. But I do! Fuck, *fuck, fuck*!'

He mother was backing away in the direction of the door. Now she was thinking of phoning the hospital. Clearly she had a madwoman in the house.

'Oh, Mummy, why don't you run away and

phone? With any luck you'll get rid of me once and for all.'

Beatrice had pulled the door open.

'Meanwhile I'll eat all my vegetables. In case that child might be harmed if I didn't.'

Beatrice threw a last terrified glance in her direction and disappeared. When Sibylla heard her hurried steps down the stairs, she ran out on the landing. She watched her mother dash across the hall in the direction of Mr Forsenström's study. Sibylla shouted after her.

'You forgot to answer my question!'

No response from downstairs.

Sibylla went back and faced the food-tray. Boiled carrots and peas. She grabbed the plate in both hands and flung it into the waste-paper basket.

Then she pulled out a suitcase and started packing.

She woke when he opened the door. Before she had time to do anything, he had already got down the few steps and looked around before striding across the floor. He still hadn't seen her.

She was lying very still, watching him.

Slight build, blond. Wire-rimmed spectacles.

He stepped up on the small platform below the clock, bent forward and put his face against the clock-face. He stretched out his arms towards the perimeter and in the light falling in through the glass, he looked like a crucified figure of Jesus.

Or Da Vinci's Man. Though with aerials attached. It was two minutes before twelve.

She scanned the attic, still motionless. There was a chance of reaching the door in time, but she would have to leave her things. He was standing in a dangerous position. If he lost his balance, he might fall out through the clock-face.

The seconds passed. The longer of his head-aerials made one more forward jump. She

hardly dared breathe, terrified of being discovered.

Finally he lowered his arms. The next moment
he turned and saw her. The sight scared him, she
could see that. He was not only scared but also
a little ashamed at having been seen. Neither
of them said anything, but they kept staring at
each other. His face was in the shade.

How in the name of God would she get out of
this? He didn't look very strong. On no account
must he be allowed to leave the attic before she
had talked to him. She sat up slowly, figuring
that it might look threatening if she stood up.

'What are you doing?'

Her tone had been hesitant. Although he
didn't answer at once, he seemed less tense.

'Nothing special.'

'No? It looked quite alarming from over
here.'

He shrugged his shoulders.

'What about you? What are you doing here?'

Good question. What am I doing here?

'I was just . . . having a rest.'

'Are you sleeping rough? Or something?'

She smiled. Well, well – he went straight to
the point. Usually people tried to avoid facing
the misery.

'It's not so rough here as other places.'

'Is it because you're homeless? Like, with
nowhere to live?'

Why should she deny it? Anyway, there was

no other reasonable explanation for her presence in the attic.

'You could say that.'

He stepped down from the platform.

'That's cool. I want to do that when I leave school.'

He would like to do *what*?

'Why?'

'Seems brilliant. No one asks you to do things or cares what you do.'

True enough. At least that was one aspect of being 'of no fixed abode'.

'If that's what you really want, there are better ways of going about getting it.'

He grinned.

'Tell me about it.'

She still wasn't sure that he was serious. Maybe he was just kidding her.

'Are you a junkie as well?'

'No, I'm not.'

'I thought all you people were junkies. I mean, isn't that why? That's what my Mum says.'

'Mums don't know everything.'

'Is that right?'

He said that with a sneer. She could see that he was not scared any more. He came over to her and she got up.

'Is this all you own?'

'Yes.'

He eyed the sleeping mat and the rucksack.

She watched him examining her things. He actually looked quite impressed.

'Dead cool.'

It was strange to be regarded as a model being, just for once. Still, this was enough talking about her.

'What are you doing here? Don't you know the floor is in really bad shape?'

'Yeah, live dangerously – help, help.'

He showed how little he cared by jumping up and down a couple of times. She put her hand on his arm.

'Hey, stop that. It would be a bore if you went straight through.'

'Oh, come off it.'

He pulled his arm away but stopped jumping. For a while she looked at him in silence. His turning up here suddenly was a threat, but it was still not clear how serious it was. She must find that out before he left. She picked up a crumpled copy of some pupils' handout from the floor, just to make her question seem more casual.

'Do you come here a lot?'

He paused before answering.

'Only sometimes.'

He was lying, but she couldn't figure out why.

'Which year are you in?'

'Fifth.'

'What about the rest of the class? When are your mates turning up?'

He shook his head. It dawned on her that he was alone. He comes here, but no one else.

'It's you who fixed the screws in the lock, isn't it?'

He inhaled at the same time as he spoke.

'Yup.'

She understood now. This was not one of the sheep, but another goat. Yet one more who had already been excluded from the homogenous mass.

'So what kind of person are you? Do you like school?'

He stared at her, apparently fearing for her sanity.

'Yeah, of course. Fantastic.'

No, in other words. Kids did this irony thing a lot nowadays, or at least the few she'd been talking to did. He kicked at a textbook on the floor. It bounced against her mat and stopped. Hello there, *Mathematics for the Fourth Form*.

'Do they give lots of benefit cash then?'

She shook her head. Was he already checking out his future rights as a homeless person?

'What do you eat and stuff? Do you root around in rubbish bins?'

He looked disgusted.

'It has happened.'

'Sick.'

'You'll have to try it if that's the future you're going in for.'

'But you get money hand-outs, don't you? Like, to buy grub and things.'

She couldn't be bothered answering. The obvious point was that if you accepted hand-outs, some people would still be in a position to tell you what you must and mustn't do. Then the school-bell rang. He seemed not to notice.

'Still, I'm not sure. Maybe I'll go for a job in TV instead.'

'Shouldn't you be off now?'

He shrugged his shudders.

'Suppose so.'

He sighed, turning to walk away.

She still wasn't convinced that he would keep this to himself and the problem was acute. A straightforward question was the simplest solution.

'Are you going to tell?'

'Tell, what?'

'About me being here. Sleeping over for a bit.'

The thought had obviously never occurred to him.

'Why should I tell?'

'No special reason.'

'What's your name?'

He had walked up the few steps to the door, but turned towards her.

'Tab. You?'

'Sylla. Tab's not your real name, is it? Did you pick it yourself?'

178

He shrugged.

'Can't remember.'

'What's your real name then?'

'Give over – what's this? *Jeopardy* or something?'

She had no idea what he was talking about and waved a hand vaguely.

'I just wondered.'

He sighed, letting go of the door handle.

'Patrik. My real name is Patrik.'

She smiled and after a moment's hesitation he smiled back. He turned to the door again.

'Cheers.'

'Bye, Patrik. See you some time?'

Then he was gone.

Of course it didn't work out. She was picked up and sent home within hours of the vegetable incident.

It didn't take long for the hospital to respond. The car crunched along the gravel drive and minutes later someone rang the doorbell.

When Beatrice Forsenström opened the door, Sibylla was already sitting on the stairs, halfway down, with her suitcase next to her. No one took any notice of her.

'Thank you for coming so soon.'

Her mother opened the door wider to allow them to step inside. The younger of the two was eyeing the handsome hall, obviously impressed. Maybe he was wondering how anyone could go nuts while living in such a grand house.

Her mother went straight to the point.

'I cannot deal with her any more. She's completely impossible.'

The second man was nodding gravely.

'Do you have any idea if she has actually become psychotic again?'

'I can't be sure. Of course, she has these

outbursts, making accusations against me and although I know she mustn't upset herself, it's so difficult . . .'

Her mother covered her eyes with her hand. Sibylla heard the door to her father's study opening and his indoor shoes pad across the tiled floor. Then she could see him over the handrail. He went up to the men and shook their hands.

'Henry Forsenström.'

'Håkan Holmgren. We've come to collect Sibylla.'

He nodded and sighed.

'Best so, I think.'

Sibylla got up.

'I'm packed and ready to go.'

Everybody turned to watch her. Her mother took a step closer to her husband, who put a protective arm round her. They seemed worried that their daughter would throw some kind of fit. When she reached the bottom of the stairs the small gathering scattered to let her pass. Once outside, she turned. The male nurses hadn't moved. She addressed them politely.

'I'm sorry, are you waiting for something?'

Håkan Holmgren took a few steps towards her.

'No, we're OK. Let's go. Sure you've packed everything you need?'

Sibylla just turned and walked towards their car, opened a rear door and climbed inside.

The others joined her a little later, presumably after another briefing on her state of mind. She never saw her parents again. Her last glimpse was of them standing on the fucking tiled floor in the hall, slandering her reputation behind her back.

After a couple of days they gave her a room of her own.

The moment she entered the ward one of her fellow patients took it into her head that Sibylla was the Virgin Mary with a new baby Jesus inside her. It wasn't a problem for her, but the staff soon became utterly bored with the woman's pleading for her sins to be forgiven. Getting Sibylla out of the way seemed the most effective solution.

Delighted with the sick woman's helpful delusions, Sibylla gratefully pulled her own door shut. All she wanted was to be left in peace.

Her belly grew bigger and bigger.

Now and then a midwife would turn up, check her blood pressure and listen to the baby through some kind of inverted funnel. The growth was apparently doing all right, because the midwife didn't call often. Instead she gave Sibylla a book about pregnancy and delivery, which went straight into the drawer in her bedside table.

This time she was allowed walks on her

own in the park, because they all agreed that the exercise was good for her. She spent a few hours walking every day. The white stone buildings looked quite beautiful, at least from a distance. If she let her mind go blank, it was possible to imagine that this was the park of a great castle.

The man who wanted her to talk didn't call very often either. Maybe he had sicker patients to look after. Apparently she was no longer crazy, only pregnant. It wasn't his fault that back home it amounted to more or less the same thing.

About two weeks before the baby was due she felt her first true contraction, an intense pain as if from a hammer blow. It passed as suddenly as it had arrived. Alone in her room, she collapsed on the bed, feeling terrified. What was that?

Then the pain struck her again, fierce and relentless.

Something had broken inside her. Fluid flooded down between her legs.

This must be death. It was her punishment. Something had broken inside her and her blood was pouring out of her. Once the pain had faded she looked down at her legs. No blood. Had she peed herself? Lost her mind or something?

The pain came in a wave next time. It hurt so much she was screaming out loud. Seconds later a female nurse came rushing in and started dealing with the wet sheets. Sibylla felt ashamed.

'I'm sorry. Please, I need help. I think something's broken inside me.'

The woman just beamed at her.

'Don't worry, Sibylla. You're about to give birth – that's all. Just wait here. I'll go and phone Transport.'

She hurried away. Phone Transport? Where were they going to transport her?

'Good luck, Sibylla!' That's what they had said after pushing her stretcher into an ambulance. The words were ringing in her ears.

Now she was in another hospital, lying in bed alone in another room.

'Would you like us to call your husband?'

She had shaken her head. There was an uneasy silence.

'Is there anyone else you'd like to be with you?'

She had not answered the question, just closed her eyes and concentrated on trying to stop the next wave of pain. She didn't have a hope, of course. Nothing she could do helped against the unbearable pain racking her body. She was reduced to being just a body, possessed by an alien force intent on drilling a hole large enough to let the creature inside it get out. Her mind was out of order, her will had been dismantled, leaving her exposed to this purposeful, unstoppable process that would give her no peace until it was over.

She was about to make life.

A white clock faced her on the opposite wall. Its hands jumped forward regularly, her only reminder of a world outside that followed other laws.

The pause between each little jump seemed so long. Hours passed.

Now and then a woman would pop in to see her. She could hear another woman's screams from somewhere nearby. Had it been like this for her mother when she gave birth to Sibylla? Was that why she never really liked her daughter, didn't even accept her existence? If you caused this much pain, how can you ask to be loved?

When the minute hand had jumped round the clock-face four times and she was almost unconscious from the effort, a new woman came to see her. Once more the visitor stuck her fingers in there, but this time it was apparently different. Her opening was ten centimetres. It sounded like a mistake, the cleft in there must be vast. Her body couldn't hold together any more. It had fallen apart, dissolved.

She was lifted onto a delivery chair. Once seated there, spread-eagled, legs wide apart and her genitals on full show, she was told to push. She was anxious to please them, but it seemed obvious that pushing would finally make her split in half. Her head would split too, right round from her chin to the back of her neck. She was pleading with them to stop the pain, but they were all in the service of the force and wouldn't let her off.

Someone said she could see the head. She told Sibylla to relax and stop pushing.

A head?

They could see a head. Coming out of her.

Once more now, Sibylla. Then it's over.

Suddenly the room echoed with a baby's crying. The last tearing pain faded away and was gone, as abruptly as it had come.

She turned to see a small dark head resting on the shoulder of a nurse, who was swiftly leaving the room.

The minute hand did another of its little jumps, just as if nothing special had happened. But a person had just emerged from inside her. A tiny human being with a head covered in dark hair. Unbidden, this creature had started growing inside her and then dynamited its way out.

Sibylla was still sitting in the seat, her head leaning heavily against the backrest and her legs wide apart. She watched as the clock registered the passing of another minute, wondering why no one had ever asked her if she minded.

In the chilly attic, the large hands rotated round and round the white clock-face and day followed night followed day.

She had found a shower-room that wasn't locked and crept down to have a hot shower every night. Standing for a long time under the water helped to thaw her body, but did not shift her depression.

When her unexpected visitor had left, the first instinct had been to pack up and leave. But then, where would she go? Her helplessness exhausted her so much she stayed where she was.

She didn't care. Let what happens happen.

She took just one additional precaution by hiding her things and rolling out her mat in the corner by the chimney-shaft. It was further from the door, but on the other hand she was less likely to be taken by surprise again.

He came back on the third day after his first

visit. Lying very still, she listened as the door opened and closed.

'Sylla?'

So it was the boy. But she couldn't see the door, so there might be someone with him.

'Sylla? It's Tab. OK, Patrik. Where are you?'

She peeped round the chimney-shaft. He was alone.

His face lit up when he saw her.

'Great. I thought maybe you'd moved on.'

She sighed and got up.

'I thought about it, believe me, but there aren't that many free pitches.'

Then she noticed that he was carrying a bulging rucksack and held a rolled-up mat under his arm.

'Off some place?'

'I'm staying here.'

'Here?'

'Sure. I'm shacking up here tonight, if that's OK by you?'

She shook her head helplessly.

'Why yes – but why?'

'It's cool. I want to experience it.'

She sighed, looking around the attic.

'Patrik, this isn't a game. I don't sleep here because it's a fun thing to do.'

'What's your reason then?'

This was irritating.

'The reason is that I've got nowhere else to go just now.'

He must have felt that she needed persuading and got something out from his rucksack. It was a grill-bag.

'Spare-ribs. Would you like some?'

She had to smile at the way he had brought her a bribe. He asked again, his head a little to the side.

'Please, can I stay here tonight?'

She shrugged.

'I can't stop you, I suppose. But what would your parents say to your sleeping rough?'

'Never mind.'

This worried her. Christ, he might have told his parents of his plans.

'Do they know where you are?'

Now he was looking at her with eyes that said how-thick-can-you-be.

'Dad's out driving his taxi all night and Mum's away on some kind of course.'

'Does anybody else know that you're here?'

He sighed.

'You're so fucking anxious. No, no one knows where I am.'

Anxious? You'd be anxious too, if only you knew where your bit of harmless fun would get you. Boyo, you're about to share a night in an attic with a wanted serial killer, probably a religious maniac.

'Fine. No problem. You're welcome.'

He didn't need to be asked twice, deciding quickly to spread out his sleeping mat on the platform in front of the great clock. She thought it better to be able to keep an eye on him and pulled her own mat to the other side of the chimney-shaft. He examined his handiwork with satisfaction and then sat down, looking at her expectantly.

'Are you hungry? Would you like some of this stuff?'

Couldn't deny that. Baked beans had its limitations.

'Sure, if you've got enough.'

He tore open the bag and spread it out on the floor between them. Then he added ready-made potato salad, two cans of Coke and two bags of crisps.

'Help yourself.'

What a feast! She came and sat next to him. He seemed to be just as hungry as she was and they ate in silence. Each spare-rib was gnawed down to the bone before being put back in the bag next to the uneaten ribs. When the two piles were almost the same height, she was so full it seemed impossible to eat a thing more. She leaned back against the wall.

He sounded surprised.

'Are you done already? I bought double helpings.'

'That's nice of you. We'll keep some for tomorrow.'

His mouth was still full.

'Maybe your stomach has shrunk. Seemingly it does if you don't get much food.'

Fascinating. Sounded true, too. He must have been used to eating his fill, because he immediately started on another spare-rib. By now, even his cheeks were smeared with oil.

'Shit. Where do you go to wash?'

Sibylla shrugged. 'If you're homeless you've got to get used to mess. Running water is sheer luxury.'

He stared at his sticky hands. Then he looked at her hands. She held them up in front of him. Only her thumb and index finger on one hand had touched the food. He quickly licked his fingers and wiped them on the legs of his trousers. Then he looked around.

'Right. Now what?'

'Now what – what?'

'I mean, you can't just . . . like, sit here? What do you usually do?'

Ah, the little person inside that almost fully-grown body is quite clueless.

'What do you usually do? When you don't hole up in attics and play at being homeless?'

'Mess around with my computer, I suppose.'

She nodded and drank some Coke.

'Not so easy if you've got nowhere to stay.'

He grinned.

'Maybe ogling the telly's the answer, then.'

She went back to her corner and crawled into her sleeping bag, sticking her hands into her armpits to keep them warm. Then she turned her head to watch him.

He was obviously bored. Already. Failing other distractions, he had started tidying up after their meal. The clock behind him showed ten minutes past six.

When he had finished clearing up, he rolled out his sleeping bag and followed her example. It was a cheap model, which meant that he would be cold during the night. That was helpful. He might leave her alone after that.

He was lying on his back with his hands under his head.

'Why did you become homeless? Haven't you ever lived any place?'

She sighed.

'I did live somewhere once.'

'Where?'

'Somewhere in Småland.'

'Why did you leave?'

'It's a long story.'

He turned his head and looked at her.

'Go ahead, I'd like to hear it. It's not as if, like, we're in a hurry.'

They had supported her in the shower afterwards and then wheeled her across to the maternity ward. In four of the five beds in the room sat recently delivered mothers with their babies. They all greeted her pleasantly when she was placed in a bed next to the window, but she immediately rolled over on her side. The window had blue-and-white striped curtains. A small border had come off the bottom of one of them. Looking out meant that she didn't have to see them, but she couldn't keep out the sounds.

Initially, no one asked her anything. They were all preoccupied with minding their own new-born babies.

She had been longing to sleep on her front, but it was still impossible. Her belly was still really big, even though it was empty. She could sense its sudden emptiness. Her breasts were aching.

They came to see her after about an hour. First, they got her to sit up, then stand and walk. Walking hurt. She could feel the tense pain from the stitches they'd used to sew her up with. Or at least, that's what they said it was.

Next, she was to speak with the doctor. She decided to stand instead of accepting his offer of a chair. He nodded at her and started leafing through her notes.

'Now Sibylla, this seems to have gone very well.'

She said nothing and he looked up at her quickly, before returning to the brown folder.

'Tell me, how are feeling?'

Empty, hollow. Used up and abandoned.

'What was it?'

He looked up again.

'Was what?'

'The baby, what kind was it?'

This bothered him, maybe because he was the one meant to ask the questions.

'A male.'

He bent over the notes.

A little boy. She had given birth to a little boy with dark hair.

'Please, can't I see him?'

He cleared his throat, apparently displeased with her unexpected line of talk.

'No, I'm afraid not. It's routine here, nothing personal. In cases such as yours, it has proved to be the best policy. For the mother's own sake, you see.'

Ah yes, for her sake. Why didn't it ever occur to anyone that she should be asked about what was best for her? How come they all knew already what was best?

He quickly finished their talk. When she returned to her room, the women were smiling in welcome. A nurse helped her into bed and she turned her back on all of them.

During the afternoon visiting-hour, fathers and relations and friends poured into the room to admire the babies. The visitors pretended not to see her back.

In the evening, only the mother in the next bed had an unbroken night's sleep. Maternal duties kept the rest of them awake. She heard them chatting quietly about their babies. He cries such a lot, I think it's his slow bowels. She always prefers the left breast – knows what she wants already, little madam. Look, he almost smiled, isn't he lovely!

She slowly got out of bed. If she hauled herself up sideways, it only hurt just before her feet took her weight.

The corridor outside was empty. She walked past the window to the nurses' station without anybody noticing her. The babies slept next door. She looked into the babies' room and it was empty apart from one plastic box on wheels in the middle of the floor. It was a baby-carrier of the kind that was wheeled along to the other mothers in the ward. Her heart was pounding as she cautiously closed the door behind her and tiptoed into the room.

A little head.

A tiny head, covered in dark hair. This was her child. Now she was trembling all over. Looking intently into the cot, she saw her baby's ID number on the note behind his head.

Her son.

She slapped her hands over her mouth to stop herself from moaning aloud. He had been part of her and had grown inside her. Now he was lying there, all alone. She had abandoned her baby boy.

He was so very tiny, lying there on his side sleeping. She could have made a pillow for his head with the palm of her hand. Gently, with one finger, she stroked the dark hair. He twitched and drew a deep breath, making a little noise like a sob. She bent over him, putting her nose to his ear.

This was intolerable. The emotion was welling up suddenly inside her.

They shouldn't have been allowed to do this, not for any reason. He was her child. They would have to kill her before she let him go. She knew with her whole being that she could never betray him, never abandon him. Never leave him alone in a plastic box crying himself to sleep.

Now she had become more courageous. She

slid her hands carefully underneath his small body and lifted him. She held him close, very close, feeling that this was how it should be.

He stayed asleep. She inhaled his baby smell with the tears running down her cheeks. She was cradling her little boy in her arms. Now she was no longer alone.

The door opened.

'What are you doing?'

She stayed where she was. She recognised the nurse, who had helped her into the doctor's room earlier that day.

'Sibylla, you must put the baby down. Come on. Let's go back to the ward now.'

'He's my son.'

The nurse seemed uncertain about what to do, but reached out her arms in order to take the baby away. Sibylla turned her back.

'I'm not letting go of him.'

Now she felt the other woman's hand on her shoulder. She shrugged to get free and the movement woke the child in her arms. He whined a little, but stopped when she gently stroked his head.

'Hush, hush my darling. Mummy's here.'

The nurse was on her way out of the room. Sibylla put her hand behind his head to get a better look at his face. His eyes had opened, small dark blue eyes moving about in order to find something to focus on.

A moment later, they were back. Four of

them this time and one of them was a man. He walked straight up to Sibylla and spoke to her authoritatively.

'Put the baby down now.'

'He's my baby.'

The man hesitated for a moment, Then he pulled out a chair for her.

'Why don't you sit down?'

'No thanks. Sitting still hurts.'

One of the others came up to her.

'Listen, Sibylla, behaving like this doesn't solve anything. You're just making it worse for yourself.'

'Worse? How?'

They looked at each other in turn. One of them left the room.

'Sibylla, everyone has agreed the child is to be adopted. He'll have the best possible opportunities, so you mustn't worry.'

'I haven't agreed to anything. And I want to keep him.'

'Sibylla, I know it's hard and I'm sorry. There's nothing we can do about it, you know.'

They were crowding her.

Three against one and the fourth presumably on her way back. She might bring reinforcements. Everyone was against her, they were all playing in the opposing team. She was facing them alone, with only her baby on her side.

The two of them against the rest of the world. So what? She wouldn't abandon him.

The man pushed the chair away.

'There are two ways to deal with this situation. Either you put him back in his cot yourself and leave quietly. Or else we'll have to force you.'

Her heart was beating hard. They were going to take him away again.

'Please, can't you see? I'm his mother. You know that. You mustn't take him away, he's all I've got.'

The tears were coming now. Her whole body shook and her head was spinning. She closed her eyes. I shall not fall ill again. Not ill.

When she opened her eyes again, it was too late.

The man was about to leave the room, holding her son in his arms. Two other men in white clothes had arrived. They grabbed her arms.

Her child was crying. She could hear the sound disappearing down the corridor.

She never saw her son again.

'That's a fucking crime! Were they allowed to do that?'

She didn't reply. She was wondering what had made her tell the story especially since she had never even mentioned it to anyone before. Her loss had been gnawing at her all the time, like a swallowed shard of glass. Its unyielding edge had kept the wound raw, but she had never before expressed her grief in words.

Maybe she had told him because he was about the same age as her son. Or maybe because of everything – the hopelessness of it all. No more point in keeping quiet.

'But what happened afterwards?'

She hesitated. These were memories she had tried hard to forget.

'They had to lock me up. I was kept in a mental hospital for almost half a year. By then I just couldn't hack it any more.'

'Jesus . . . were you, you know, like . . . crazy?'

She couldn't be bothered answering. They sat in silence for while.

'How do you mean, couldn't hack it? Did you go on the run?'

'Yes, I did. Not that I think they chased me that much. I wasn't exactly a danger to the public.'

Not like now, that is.

'What about your Mum and Dad? What did they say?'

'Good question. Well, they said I couldn't stay with them. I was an adult and had made my own bed and could go lie in it and so on.'

'Fucking sickoes.'

Indeed.

'Then what did you do?'

She looked at him.

'Are you always this curious?'

'I've never talked to a drifter before.'

She sighed, raising her eyes to the ceiling. Well, then. Listen and learn.

'First, I went to the nearest biggish town – it was Växsjö. I was scared silly that they'd find me and send me back to the hospital. I was moving about for a couple of months or so, sleeping in basements and eating what I could find.'

'How old were you?'

'It was just after my eighteenth birthday.'

'That's three years older than me.'

'Than I.'

He turned to look at her.

'Than what?'

'You should say "older than I".'

He snorted.

'Were you a damn prefect at school or what?'

She was smiling into the darkness. No, never a prefect. They didn't pick her.

'No, but I was rather good at Swedish – at writing essays and things.'

'Why didn't you ever get a job?'

'I didn't dare tell people my name. They might recognise it, you see. I thought they were looking for me, that I was wanted by the police.'

The last phrase brought her right back to the present. Where exactly was this chat taking her? Time to cut it short, now.

'Good night.'

He lifted his head, leaning on one elbow.

'Hey, you can't stop now.'

He sounded disappointed, but she turned her face towards the wall.

'It's almost eleven o'clock and I'm tired. So, good night.'

'Please, just one more thing. How come you ended up in Stockholm? Can't you tell me about that bit, too?'

She sighed and turned again. The lamps illuminating the clock-face were throwing their white light into the attic, but its corners remained pitch dark.

'Listen, I'll only say this much. If I were you, I'd go for a job in television. You wouldn't sleep too well if I told you about everything I've seen and done and felt on the streets.'

She stopped speaking for a moment, tried to find the right words. How much of herself could she give? Then she sat up.

'Six of these years are blanks, I hardly remember a single thing. Who I was with. Where I slept. I was drunk out of my mind most of the time. I didn't want to be able to think, because if I did I might lose my grip and sink without trace. You see, living on the streets gets to you. It's really hard to pull yourself out. The main reason is that you become unable to adjust to living in other conditions. You have to be able to conform to regular society and you *don't want to* conform. It's a vicious circle. Patrik, you must listen to me. I know what it's like and you're just wrong about the freedom thing. It's a load of shit, all that about sleeping rough. You haven't got a fucking clue about what it's like, not really.'

She lay down again. For once Patrik was quiet, presumably silenced by her vehemence. Would he really stay all night? Maybe he was angry now?

Not another word. She could hear him stirring, testing different positions on the thin sleeping mat. Then the attic became totally quiet.

She felt too restless to sleep. Memory snapshots came and went behind her closed eyelids, in fast-changing sequences. His questions had ripped the lid off stored experiences that she had avoided for years.

The memories of hitchhiking to Stockholm in the hope of merging with the crowds in the capital and so find some way to earn a living. How frightened she had been all the time that they would trace her, catch her and lock her up in hospital again. As if anyone had cared about her absence!

Then came the slow realisation of how difficult it is for someone without money, contacts or even a name to find a safe harbour. She didn't dare use her ID number, which meant that the Job Centres were out of the question. She had taken some illegal jobs as a cleaner or dish-washer, but moved on as soon as anyone at all became curious about her. Safety seemed to be among those who only knew each other by nicknames and never asked any questions except about drink or drugs and only when necessary. In the end, hungry and tired to death, she had faced utter humiliation, swallowed her pride and phoned home to ask for help. Begging for forgiveness, she told them she wanted to come home again.

'We'll give you an allowance, Sibylla. If you give us your address, we'll send you the money.'

As always when she remembered this, her stomach contracted. If only she hadn't given in! She often thought that phone call was harder to bear than almost anything else she had been through. It was intolerable that when she spoke to her mother for the last time, she had been reduced to apologising yet again.

The money started arriving. Because she had an income and spoke in dialect, her mates called her the Queen of Småland.

Her lost years began. She spent all her energy on staying intoxicated for as much of the time as possible. Nothing else mattered. With her brain activity permanently set on Low, most things became endurable. There was even a sense of security to be gained from the degradation that meant nothing was questioned and nothing was unacceptable. Slowly but surely she adjusted to the more or less overt contempt of people she encountered. The recognition that she was a loser only sealed her solidarity with the other outcasts.

For six years, this was her life – six years outside time.

Then, a turning point. It happened when she woke up on a bench near the Slussen walkway, heavily drunk, smeared with vomit and lying in a pool of her excrement. Around her stood an entire class of little primary school kids, watching her with wonder.

'Miss. What's she doing there? Is she sick?'

'Miss. Why does she smell so?'

A wall of children, all round-eyed with astonishment at this, their first insight into the downside of adulthood. The shocked teacher, who was about her own age, turned up and protectively herded her charges away.

'Come now. Don't look!'

Then a terrible thought had struck her. Her own son might have been one of the children and the state she was in was conclusive proof that her mother's decision had been right.

She turned to look at her new-found companion. It seemed that he had managed to sleep in the end. She crawled out of her sleeping bag to put her anorak over the boy. He was lying on his back with his arms crossed over his chest to keep warm.

How young he was.

His whole life ahead, unused. Somewhere her son had reached almost the same age.

She crawled back. Much longer in this attic and she'd go off her head.

Formulating this thought immediately led on to the realisation that something had happened to her – a good thing. She glanced towards her visitor again and thought that he had brought something else, much more important than spare-ribs and Coke. His respect for her as a fellow human being had granted her a new kind of dignity. For some inscrutable reason he was the one who had found her here. She was made stronger by his unreserved interest and admiration for what he felt she stood for. During the last few days some of her normal instincts had seemed damaged beyond recovery, but now they were reviving. Most of all, her instinct to fight against the odds.

The worst darkness was lifting. Tomorrow she'd pull herself together, do something.

They wouldn't crush her this time either, so there. She wondered if the nationwide search for her was still on. Better get hold of a paper.

*T*hen I saw a new Heaven and a new Earth;
for the first Heaven and the first Earth had
passed away and the sea was no more. And I
saw the Holy City, a New Jerusalem, coming
down out of Heaven from God, prepared as a
bride adorned for her husband; and from afar
I heard a great voice from the throne saying:

'Behold, the dwelling of God is with men.
He will dwell with them and they shall be His
people, and God himself will be with them; He
will wipe away every tear from their eyes and
death shall be no more, neither shall there be
mourning nor crying nor pain any more, for
former things have passed away.'

And He who sat upon the throne said:

'Behold, I make all things new.' Also he
said:

'Write this down for these words are trust-
worthy and true.'

And He said to me:

'It is done. I am the Alpha and Omega, the
beginning and the end. To the thirsty I will
give water without price from the fountain

*of the water of life. He who conquers shall
have this heritage and I will be his God and
he shall be my son. But as for the cowardly,
the faithless, the polluted, as for murderers,
fornicators, sorcerers and idolaters and all liars,
their lot shall be in the lake that burns with fire
and brimstone, which is the second death.'*

Lord, I have done my duty.
  Now, all I can do is wait.

She had been surreptitiously watching him for a long time before he woke. The cold must have troubled him during the night, because he'd put her anorak on.

During the small hours, she had made up her mind. She needed his help. Her only hope lay in telling him the truth. Then she went over what she must say again and again, trying to find the most gentle way to describe her situation.

When he woke his first move was to reach for his glasses. Then he sat up and looked at her, pulling his sleeping bag tightly around him.

'It's so fucking cold. Thanks for the anorak, it's great. Do you want it back now?'

'You keep it. My sleeping bag is warmer than yours.'

The clock behind him showed ten minutes past nine.

'When do you start school?'

He smiled at her.

'Knock, knock, anybody in? It's Saturday.'

She smiled too. It was nice to be made fun of

like that. His hand emerged from the sleeping bag again, aiming for the grill-bag. He put it in his lap and opened it.

'Urrgh. Spare ribs for breakfast!'

'Do you want some of my crisp-bread? I've got some yoghurt too.'

He liked the idea and shoved the grill-bag back on the floor. Still wrapped in the sleeping bag he hopped across to her.

'Hey, take it easy. The floor could break.'

'Yeah?'

When he reached her, he settled with a thump. She shook her head and he grinned at her, grabbing a slice of crisp-bread.

He must have been really hungry. When he was wolfing his seventh slice she put the packet away.

'Tomorrow's another day.'

'We'll buy some more. No problem.'

She just looked at him and he grimaced, obviously realising how silly he had been.

'Sorry. I'll buy it. I'll give you the money, if you like.'

'Thanks, but no thanks.'

This was the right moment. How should she best open up the subject? She steeled herself, taking a deep breath.

'Do you follow the news, read the papers?'

He shrugged.

'Not a lot. Mum wants me to read a proper paper like *Dagens Nyheter*, but it's way too much. Takes hours getting through it. But I do check out *The Express*. Dad brings it back after work. Why? Do you? Read a newspaper, I mean.'

'I do when I can. When I find one lying about. Or else I go to the Culture House. The reading room there has all the dailies.'

This was clearly news to him, but he nodded knowingly. She carried on talking.

'Yesterday, did you look at the papers?'

He shook his head at first.

'Wait, I did. The *DN* Friday supplement.'

How should she handle this? Did she have the right to involve him? It had seemed perfectly reasonable while he was asleep.

'Patrik, have you ever been accused of doing something you didn't do?'

'Suppose so. Have you got some yoghurt, or . . . ?'

She sighed and produced her big container.

'Thanks. Can I have it straight from the pack?'

'Sure. Unless you brought a nice plate, of course.'

He grinned and she started again. The introductory bit was the hardest.

'I have, you see – been accused of something I didn't do, that is.'

He seemed focused on the yoghurt. Drinking it was hard, it was really too thick. He kept tapping the bottom of the pack.

'Does the name Sibylla mean anything to you?'

He nodded, but still seemed more interested in the yoghurt.

'Patrik, you mustn't feel bad about this. Be cool.'

She hesitated for one more brief moment.

'I'm Sibylla, you see.'

He didn't react first. Then the penny dropped. He stiffened, put the yoghurt down and turned to look at her. There was real fear in his eyes.

'Please, believe me, I didn't do it. I just happened to be in the Grand Hotel when someone killed that guy. I'm innocent.'

He was clearly unconvinced. His eyes flickered round the attic for a moment, as if seeking an escape route. She must gain time. Somehow this wasn't working out the way she'd hoped. The words came spontaneously now, not in the careful order she had practised.

'Oh, for Christ's sake, Of course I'm not a serial killer. You wouldn't have been sitting here now if I had been, after all I've had all night to chop you up into little pieces.'

This was not a good way of putting it. In fact, it was pretty disastrous. Suddenly he made a move to get away, but the sleeping bag trapped him.

He mustn't go – not yet.

She leapt at him, pinning him down against the mat with her knees on his arms. His quick

213

breathing sounded like sobbing. His tears were not far away.

Oh God no!

'Please. Don't hurt me.'

She closed her eyes. What was she doing?

'You must know that I won't hurt you. Please listen to me. I'm holed up in this freezing attic with every single cop in the country after me. They've made up their minds that I'm it. I haven't got a chance. Like I said yesterday, people like me have no rights. Oh Patrik, you've got to believe me. I told you all that personal stuff yesterday because I trusted you. I thought you at least would believe in me.'

By now the sobs had quietened down.

'I'm telling you this because I need your help. I don't dare go into a shop even.'

His wide, frightened eyes were fixed on her. She sighed.

'OK, I'm sorry. Forgive me.'

Just imagine what anybody watching them would make of her sitting astride a defence-less fifteen year-old. She stood up, letting him go.

'Go away now.'

He stayed where he was, very still and looking as if he hardly dared to breathe.

'Go!'

He twitched in response to her loud voice. Then he crawled out of his sleeping bag and started slowly walking towards the door, his back tense as if he feared she would jump on him from behind.

'I need my anorak.'

He stopped at once, let the anorak slide to the floor and walked on. When he reached the door he suddenly leapt at it and rushed out. She could hear his running footsteps in the corridor outside.

Slumping down on her mat, she knew staying in the attic was not possible now. She had to leave, at once. She packed his things neatly and then started on her own. A few minutes later everything was tidied away. Just inside the door, she turned to cast a last glance at the clock. Bye, bye.

Into the corridor, down the stairs. On the ground floor she stopped for a moment. The mere thought of opening the door to the world outside made her feel sick. This everlasting fear would destroy her in the end. She chose to walk round to the back door leading into the school-yard. The thought of the street was too frightening.

The door slammed behind her, shutting her off from her refuge for good. Crossing the yard, she walked towards the Vitaberg Park. She had no idea what to do next. Then she heard someone shouting behind her. The sound alarmed her and she stopped, looking around for somewhere to hide.

'Sylla! Wait!'

Then she saw him come running round the corner and waited until he reached her. At first he didn't speak and she started to walk off.

'I'm sorry I didn't believe you at first, but I was so fucking scared.'

He was a little breathless. She turned to look at him and discovered a new expression in his eyes, a seriousness that she had not seen before. Then he stared at the ground, as if ashamed by his own admission of fear.

'Don't worry about it.'

'No, it's because I know you're speaking the truth, Sylla.'

She kept walking, unable to bear the thought of starting to plead with him again.

He hurried after her.

'Sylla, please. You see, I saw the news on the poster in the Co-op window.'

She stopped. He was obviously trying hard to choose the right words.

'The story is that you murdered someone else last night.'

S he felt uneasy.

'Are you absolutely sure he's asleep?'

Patrik sounded impatient.

'Relax. He's on nightshifts and doesn't usually wake up until the afternoon.'

She was feeling uncomfortable. What would his father do if he found a woman with unnaturally jet-black hair, camping with her rucksack in his son's room? Old enough to be his mother, too.

They were in the block of flats where Patrik lived, whispering together at the bottom of the stairs.

'And your mother, are you sure – really sure, sure – that she isn't coming home?'

'Sure. Not until tomorrow night.'

Maybe he was right but then, maybe he wasn't. Besides, was it really right to involve him?

When she learned the latest news she'd had to go and sit down on the nearest park bench. He had followed her silently, leaving her in peace.

Sitting there looking out over the empty school-yard, she felt her courage ebbing away again. Staring at the large clock-face, she thought she should have followed her impulse of a few nights ago and made the school attic her last resting-place.

He tried to say something hopeful to cheer her up.

'Listen. I can tell the police you were with me all last night.'

She only snorted at that, but then felt guilty because it had sounded like a put-down.

'They would just have added pederasty to my list of crimes.'

He sounded grumpy.

'I happen to be fifteen years old. Actually.'

What's the answer to that?

'Patrik, I've had it. I might as well confess and put an end to the whole saga.'

'Shit, no! Don't!'

He was really upset.

'Listen, you can't confess to something you haven't done!'

'What do you suggest then?'

'Can't you go there and . . . like, talk to them?'

'Same difference.'

'I don't get it. Why?'

'Surely you can see that? The police have already made up their minds. I *am* the murderer. They won't believe a thing I say.'

She put her head in her hands, speaking quietly to the ground in front of her.

'Worse, I can't hack being locked up.'

He sounded less convinced now.

'But you're just telling them what really happened.'

Then she told him about Jörgen Grundberg. About how her fingerprints got on to his keycard, about the wig and the Swiss army knife she'd left behind in the hotel room. About everything in her past that had combined to make her the prime suspect. Former patient in a mental hospital, homeless and without any kind of social network, she was so utterly perfect that the police must be rubbing their hands with glee. No question about her guilt.

Anyway, to have a chance of finally persuading them of her innocence, they would have to keep her under lock and key for the duration of the inquiry. That would drive her insane. She had been there before and knew what she was talking about.

'The murderer has got the idea too. I'm a perfect scapegoat for him. He even left a confession in my name after the Västervik murder.'

He nodded gently.

'He did the same in Bollnäs.'

'Was that where he struck last night?'

'The night before. I don't know where he was last night.'

She was slumped against the backrest of the

bench. The night before last as well, while she was tucked up in the attic. Now they suspected her of four murders.

He stared at her.

'You didn't know, did you?'

She sighed.

'No. I didn't.'

Silence. He was thinking. The complications must be dawning on him.

'I know. Let's go to my house and check everything they've written about you.'

'How do you mean?'

'We'll surf the net.'

Ah, the Internet. She had read about it in the papers, a fantastic new world she knew nothing about. She felt as doubtful about it as she did about being invited home by this helpful fifteen-year-old.

'Why would that be any good?'

'Maybe we'll find something that proves it couldn't have been you. I bet you haven't read everything they've written.'

'Right enough.'

He got up.

'Let's go.'

What other option was there?

They crept through the hall. She felt like a thief and her heart was pounding.

'This way.'

They were outside a door in his flat. A metal

sign had been stuck on it. It said: ENTER AT
YOUR OWN RISK.

Fine. She hadn't wanted to come here in the
first place.

They passed an open doorway to a spacious living room and then the closed door
to his parents' bedroom. Patrik had put his
finger to his lips as a signal to be quiet. His
father was asleep in there. Then Patrik opened
the door to his room and waved her on. All
this was very awkward, but she followed to
please him.

His room looked as if it had been in the path
of a storm-force gale. The floor was practically
invisible under a tidal wave of clothes, old
comics, CD boxes and books. She dumped
her rucksack in the middle of it all, looking
quizzically at him.

'I know, I promised Mum to keep my room
tidy. I just kind of forget.'

'Tell me about it.'

They were speaking in whispers.

He pushed a button on the PC and when it
came alive with a little melody, she told him to
turn it down. While the computer started up,
she looked around the room. Apart from the
desk, there was an unmade bed and a bookshelf.
She pulled the cover over the bed to make the
place look less messy.

When the screen on his desk had filled with
symbols, he sat down to work. She wandered

across to an apparently empty aquarium by the window, because something moved inside it.

'That's Batman, my Greek land-tortoise.'

Batman had crawled into a corner to munch on a lettuce leaf. He looked quite content, so the world must seem quite agreeable to his tiny mind. She felt momentarily envious.

Patrik was using the keypad to write something.

serial killer sibylla

He clicked, the computer started working and after a few seconds produced the results. 67 hits. He was smiling.

'Great.'

'What does it all mean?'

'We've got 67 pages to search for stuff about you and your manic killing spree.'

She was amazed at having become unwittingly a part of this strange 'online' world that she had been reading about. Patrik was already scrolling through what looked like pictures of newsprint.

'I'll print the lot and then we can read it when we like.'

It was all new and weird to her, but he seemed to know what he was doing. Already another machine on the table had started humming and spitting out paper. The print was on the side she couldn't see but she grabbed the first lot of papers and settled down on the bed.

Meanwhile, Patrik kept clicking and feeding more paper into the printer.

The first sheet began with an eye-catching headline.

GRAND HOTEL WOMAN BREAKS THE WIDOW'S PEACE

Lena Grundberg has curled up in the sofa in her comfy sitting room. She is meeting us at home in the house where she lived with her beloved husband Jörgen until less than a week ago. Last Thursday he was the first victim of a cold-blooded murder. The deranged killer from Grand Hotel appears to be a 32-year-old woman, who so far has managed to disappear without trace in spite of a nationwide police search. But only two days after the bestial murder at the Grand, the madwoman visited the grieving widow.

Lena could hardly keep her tears back as she tells us her story.

'I'm so terribly afraid all the time,' she confessed. 'This woman just rang the doorbell and then she told me a lot of lies about how she'd just lost her husband. I never understood what she wanted, but when I later saw the police reconstruction I recognised her face at once . . .

Sibylla stopped reading. What a pack of lies! The grieving widow couldn't hold back her tears. Is that so? Screw her.

By now there was a new pile of printouts. She grabbed the lot.

ANATOMICAL KNOWLEDGE IS A COMMON SKILL FOR SLAUGHTER KILLERS

The police are baffled by the case of the 32-year-old woman, who has been charged in her absence for several murders in which the victims were butchered. A study of all 'butchery' murders carried out in Sweden since the 1960s shows that the murderer typically belongs to occupational groups such as doctors, veterinarians, hunters and butchers. According to Sten Bergman, professor of Forensic Psychiatry, this is a consequence partly of the fact that these professionals have overcome the fear of dissection felt by most people and partly because they have the technical skills.

According to the police investigation of the 32-year-old woman's past, nothing in her background fits with these occupational statistics. Of course, more than just the mental and physical skills are required to turn a person into a potential killer of this kind. Above all, they often have a mental defect associated with low empathy and strong contempt for other people.

Severe mental illness with delusions is another likely precondition. For instance, it seems that in some cases the murderer cannot bear to separate from his or her victim, something that seems to be the case with the 32-year-old woman. In this frame of mind, the perpetrator feels that he or she must have a trophy as a memento of the dead person or of the act of killing. Such personalities believe that they are in control of life and death.

The victims have been subjected to mutilations, which fit a pattern described as 'aggressive'. This is different from so-called passive butchery, carried out in order to conceal the nature of the crime or complicate later investigations. There is no evidence of this kind of precautionary approach in any of her murders. The woman's only intention has been to desecrate her victims. The police are still unwilling to disclose what she did or which body parts she had . . .

She rose, throwing the papers on the floor.

'It's too much. I can't read any more.'

She had raised her voice and Patrik turned to look at her.

'Hey, quiet!'

She sat down again, listening to the machine spitting out many more sheets of print. People had written all that, thinking about her. Nobody had paid any attention to her before and now she was suddenly the most written-about person in Sweden.

It was so fucking hateful.

'Can't stay here. I'm off.'

He turned her way again.

'Oh, yeah? Like, to where?'

She sighed.

The click of a door opening was heard from somewhere in the flat. They looked anxiously at each other, listening intently. They could hear the rushing water when a tap was turned on. Sibylla rose, looking for places to hide.

'Relax, he's probably just in the loo.'

Patrik wasn't reassuring enough. The moment the tap stopped running she dived down under the bed, just before there was a knock on the door.

'You in there, Patrik?'

No reply. Sibylla saw his feet disappear and heard him lie down on the bed. The door opened and a pair of naked hairy legs walked in.

'What, are you asleep?'

'Kind of.'

'It's past eleven o'clock, you know.'

The machine on the desk made a humming noise, producing a belated printout.

'What's that?'

The hairy legs stepped closer. The next second, Patrik's jeans-clad legs materialised right in front of her nose. He must have grabbed the paper.

'Just some stuff.'

'Stuff, eh? And why are you in bed with your clothes on?'

'I was up, really. I felt like lying down for a bit.'

'Ah. What are you printing?'

'I've been surfing a bit. Nothing special.'

The silence lasted for a few unbearable seconds.

'Well, I'm going back to bed now. Are you at home today, or what?'

'Maybe. I'm not sure.'

'If you go out, please don't come back later than ten o'clock. And you must phone to say where you are.'

She could hear Patrik sighing. The naked male legs walked towards the door and then stopped.

'That's not your rucksack, is it?'

Sibylla closed her eyes, while Patrik seemed to take an age replying. Christ, just say something. You've found it. Nicked it. Any bloody thing at all.

'It's Viktor's.'

That's a good one.

'What's it doing here?'

'He forgot it in school and I promised to look after it.'

Better still. The legs were walking again.

'See you later. Remember, you must tidy up in here before your Mum comes back.'

'I will.'

Then the door finally closed behind him and Patrik's smiling face was peering at her below the edge of the bed.

'Were you scared then?'

She crawled out. She tried to brush the dust off her front while she hissed at him,

'Can't you lock the door?'

He was sitting on the bed studying the piece of paper he had hidden from his Dad. She looked over his shoulder.

HUNTING A KILLER.

He seemed thoughtful.

'I know what we've got to do.'

She couldn't think what to say.

'Think! The police are after you and nobody else. Question: who's to track down the real murderer?'

No idea.

'Don't you see? We'll have to do it. We've got to find the murderer.'

At first she felt simply angry. So angry that she started towards the door, picking up her rucksack in the passing. She stopped with her hand reaching for the door handle, suddenly uncertain. She didn't dare step outside yet.

She put the rucksack down and sighed.

'Patrik, don't be silly. This isn't some kind of exciting game.'

'I know. It's just – well, do you have any better ideas?'

She turned to face him, but he was picking up the papers she had thrown down. She went to help him and when the papers were stacked in order again, she sat down on the bed.

'What chances do you think we've got?'

He leaned forward, speaking in an eager whisper.

'Sylla, listen. The police are looking for *you*. No one else. It gives us space. We know that there must be another person who's the killer.'

'So what can we do? We've no information.'

He looked up and met her eyes.

'Please promise not to be angry.'

'What? I mean, how can I promise?'

He hesitated. By now she was truly curious about what it was that he thought might make her angry.

'Ah . . . my Mum's in the police.'

She was transfixed. He met her eyes. When the full significance of what he had said dawned on her, her blood seemed to pump faster through her body and she rose.

'I've got to get out of here. Check the hall, please.'

'Cool it.'

'*Now*. Please, Patrik.'

She had raised her voice to a dangerous pitch and he obeyed, sighing. After peering outside, he opened the door wide. She got hold of her rucksack and walked swiftly past him.

'Please, Sylla. Please listen!'

She was walking quickly, but he was only a few steps behind her. When she'd turned the corner and started down Folkunga Street, she hoped she'd lose him. Not one word more from Patrik. 'My Mum's in the police.' Fancy that. He had invited her straight into a hornets' nest. She stopped abruptly. He was unprepared and crashed straight into her.

'So what do you think would've happened if your Mum had come home unexpectedly. Fucking what, exactly?'

The adrenaline was still rushing through her veins.

'Come off it. She's on a course!'

She looked at him, shaking her head. He was too young to understand. Maybe she wasn't being fair on him.

'Patrik, it's my life we're discussing here. Say she'd caught the 'flu or something and returned a day early or whatever. Anything. There I would've been, in her son's bedroom. Was that what you had in mind?'

He took a few steps back. He looked angry.

'Right. Fine. You don't trust me. Why don't you go and get pissed then? That's the best you can do, isn't it?'

Suddenly her anger melted away. He was her only real friend and here she was, ditching him. It was a chilly day and he hadn't had time to fetch a jacket. He was wrapping his arms round his chest to keep warm.

It seemed impossible to think of a way forward. It wasn't as if it hadn't been hard before, but now she felt responsible for this youngster as well. Of course there was no telling what he might do as soon as he got out of sight, but she had only herself to blame. She had dragged him into this mess. She sighed, really deeply this time.

'Go home. Find yourself a thick jacket.'

He looked suspicious.

'Yeah? Why?'

'Simple. You're feeling the cold.'

'Aha. Don't you think I get your cunning plan? Like, when I come back you'll be gone.'

'Then what?'

Their eyes met.

He thought of something, pulled his wallet from his jeans and put it in the pocket of her anorak.

'Look after it until I come back.'

In seconds he had disappeared round the corner. That was a clever move. The kid wasn't stupid. He'd do well. She got hold of his wallet, weighing it in her hand.

Then she closed her eyes and couldn't help smiling.

He was still not entirely convinced that she would stay put.

'I'll be hanging about just outside, in Björn's Garden.'

She realised how uncertain he felt.

'I promise, I'll be here.'

She really meant it this time. He nodded and walked off across Göt Street. She watched him until he'd disappeared out through the doors of the Citizen Place library.

He had returned wearing his jacket. When he saw her, his face broke into a happy smile that would have enchanted any mad killer on the run. She smiled back, listening gravely as he outlined his plan.

First, he would email the police, giving her an alibi for the night of the last murder. She baulked at that and urged him not to give away where they had been and – above all – not to reveal who he was. While she was saying all that, she found him looking at her with his how-fucking-stupid-do-you-think-I-am? look on his face. Then he pointed out that if he had wanted to let them know who he was, all he needed to do was to email from his home computer. He had planned to protect his identity by using the library terminal, of course.

So she left him to it and went outside to wait for him in Björn's Garden. Citizen Place was full of Saturday afternoon strollers, but there were no familiar faces among the people on the seats round the central square. Thank God.

He joined her barely ten minutes later.

'What did you tell them?'

'I told them that they'd find Sibylla Forsenström sitting on a seat in Citizen Place right now. But not to worry their heads about it 'cause she's innocent.'

For just one fraction of a second, she believed him. Then she inhaled deeply.

'Patrik. That wasn't even a little funny.'

'I didn't think you'd laugh. What I actually said was that I wanted to remain anonymous, but I knew that you were not the killer. One hundred per cent certain.'

A thought struck her.

'So how can you be sure? I could've murdered the rest of them. All you know is that I wasn't out killing people last night.'

'Bah. So you're super dangerous? Who do you think you're kidding?'

She insisted.

'Seriously, though. What if it's me?'

He screwed up his eyes thoughtfully.

'And? Are you?'

She waited for a fraction of a second, then she smiled and looked into his eyes.

'No. But look, you're not entirely sure.'

'Of course I am – it's just that you're going on and on about not trusting you.'

He was a little irritated, but so was she. She had no intention of becoming an exciting fantasy figure for him to play games with for a while.

'I simply don't want you to take things for granted.'

He looked mostly bewildered now, clearly not seeing her point. Good, good. It meant that she was still in control, which was how she wanted it.

They sat in silence side by side, thinking and watching the people walking past. No one paid any attention to the odd couple on the bench.

Then two police cars came swooping along at top speed but using only their blue lamps to clear the traffic. The sirens were switched off. Both cars pulled up in front of the library and, from each car, two constables leapt out and rushed into the building.

Time to go.

Exchanging a glance, they got up and hurried down Tjärhov Street. Then they climbed the slope toward Mosebacke Square and, still without speaking, settled down on one of the benches. The sun chose this moment to break through the solid grey cloud that for days had been in place over the city like a lid. Sibylla leaned back and closed her eyes. Warmth and sunshine. There were countries with lots of it. She could go to one of them and no one would find her there. But no. She had not been allowed to go abroad with her parents when she was a child and now she had no chance of getting a passport.

Then he broke the long silence.

'How about I go to my Mum's office and check out her computer records?'

Well, now.

'You mustn't do anything of the sort.'

'No? I'm going to do it anyway.'

'I won't let you. You might get bogged down in all this shit and I don't want that.'

'I'm bogged down already.'

He sounded rather sharp and what he said was true enough. Still, remembering her own polite teenage self, always anxious to please and as quiet as a clam, she hadn't realised quite how enterprising he would be. She preferred to think that she would never have told him her story if she had known. On the other hand, she could have been wrong. Maybe getting a taste of law-breaking is good for young people.

'Is there any chance of you doing that without being discovered?'

'I turn up at the station and ask if she's

in. When they tell me she's away, I ask to be allowed to wait in her room.'

'But you know she's on a course.'

'The receptionist doesn't know.'

'What if she does?'

He lost patience with her lack of enthusiasm.

'Christ, I don't know. I'll think of something.'

He was far too nonchalant. Not so good.

'What if they discover you fiddling with the computer?'

'They won't.'

'*If*, I said.'

He didn't answer, just slapped his hands against his thighs and got up.

'Let's go.'

'Go where?'

His face showed what he thought about having to explain everything twice.

'My Mum's office, of course!'

She stared at him. Either he was her guardian angel sent to save her, or a demon, who would give her the final shove into the abyss. There was no telling until later.

'Would you mind if I don't tag along while you wheedle your way into police premises?'

He grinned.

'Where do we meet afterwards?'

S he hadn't heard him come. She'd been sitting on the quayside behind the City Hall, watching the hands moving round the clock-face on the Riddarholm Church. After one hour, she began to think seriously about going away.

She didn't. Half an hour later, a paper was suddenly dangled in front of her nose.

He'd crept up behind her. When she turned she saw pride glowing in his eyes behind the wire-rimmed spectacles.

She started reading. There was a list of individuals: two male and two female names. The first one was Jörgen Grundberg. The police believed that she had killed these four people.

Patrik was leaning over her shoulder.

'Look, it's all the murdered people, complete with addresses and ID numbers. Last night's victim lived in Stocksund, that's in Stockholm – isn't it?'

She nodded. Bang went her alibi. She could easily have travelled to Stocksund and back while Patrik was asleep in the school attic. Not that the thought seemed to have occurred to him yet. He was still delighted by how clever he had been.

She looked out over the Riddar Firth, where the sun was making the little waves glitter. A couple of ducks floated past.

'Hmmm. Now what?

He pulled some folded pieces of paper from his pocket.

'I printed out a few things I found.'

'Did anybody see you?'

'No. I didn't use Mum's PC after all, because Kevin next door had gone for a crap and left his logged on.'

Sibylla shook her head.

'You're crazy.'

He beamed at her.

'Kevin was away for ages. By the way, I don't think either of them – that's Kevin and my Mum – is working on this case. But there was some general info in the mailbox.'

He showed her the first sheet.

'Look, this is what the murderer is leaving behind at each site.'

It was a black and white picture of a crucifix made of dark wood with the figure of Christ apparently made of a silver-like metal. The measurements were listed with millimetre accuracy.

The next picture was a black and white photo of a wall with flowery wallpaper above an unmade bed. The bed linen had large dark stains. There was a line of carefully printed text just above the bed.

ACCURSED ARE THOSE WHO ROB THE INNOCENTS OF THEIR RIGHTS. Sibylla.

She looked up at him. He quickly handed her the last of the sheets. It was a picture of a pair of transparent plastic gloves. The text said *Nutex size 8.*

'They use these in hospitals and things.'

Really? That solves the case then.

'That's all I had time to look at. Anyway, we've got their names now.'

'Exactly what can we do with them?'

He twisted round to face her, apparently choosing his words with care.

'Do you know what I think?'

Not a clue.

'I think you seem to have packed it in. You aren't really keen to work on finding the solution. Like, you don't give a shit.'

'And is that so strange?'

'I guess not but when I do that sort of thing my Dad always says I mustn't sit there feeling sorry for myself. I must try and fix whatever instead. Do something.'

Yes. Good luck to your Dad.

'Yesterday you kept going on about how misunderstood the homeless were, and people like that. How you hadn't got a chance and you on your own and all that. But you do have a chance and you aren't fucking well taking it.'

He was getting worked up. She was looking at him with real interest. She wasn't sure if what he said was more insulting than enlightening, but it was certainly justified. She rose.

'You're right, boss. OK, let's go. What should we do, do you think?'

'Let's go to Västervik.'

'You're joking!'

'No. I've checked out the bus times already. There's one leaving Stockholm in half an hour. Four hundred and sixty kronor return. I'll lend you the money. We'll arrive at four forty and that will give us two hours and twenty minutes before we catch the bus back.'

'You *are* crazy.'

'We'll be back at quarter past eleven.'

She reached for the last straw.

'You're meant to be back home before ten.'

'Nope. I'm going to a movie, I've already phoned Dad.'

The landscape was rushing past the bus windows. She spent most of the time looking out. Södertälje. Nyköping. Norrköping. Söderköping. Patrik kept studying the police computer printouts, apparently hoping to find a hidden clue if only he examined the pictures closely enough.

She had paid for their tickets. In the seclusion of the Ladies she had taken a thousand-kronor note from her savings. When she met up with Patrik afterwards, he had bought two bags of crisps and a two-litre bottle of Coke. His eyes grew round with surprise when she got the tickets, but asked no questions.

She liked that.

'Why are you getting involved in all this, really?'

He shrugged.

'It freaks me out.'

She wasn't going to let him get off so easily.

'Seriously, though. Have you nothing better

to do than hang out with an old hag of thirty-two?'

He grinned at her.

'You only thirty-two?'

Pointless question. He must have read her age hundreds of times in the newspapers. She kept looking at him, until finally he folded his bits of paper and put them away in an inside pocket.

'I just don't get it, I mean this thing about always joining some group. Mum and Dad go on about it non-stop. I can't help it if I don't fancy arsing about playing hockey or football and whatever. It just so happens I don't give a shit who gets into the Premier League. So what?'

She nodded apologetically.

'Fine. I just wondered.'

She went back to staring out the window again and he returned to his bits of paper.

The Västervik murder victim had been a Sören Strömberg, ID 36 02 07-4639. They were going to find his nearest and dearest. She remembered well how she had travelled to see Lena Grundberg, full of courage and hope.

How differently she felt now.

The bus was on time. She kept in the background while Patrik asked the girl in the bus terminal shop for directions to Siver Street, Strömberg's address.

It wasn't far to go. By the time they were

nearly there, she was feeling very uneasy. Patrik was hurrying ahead, unworried and enthusiastic, as if on his way to a good party.

It was a two-storey house with a mansard roof. Someone had chosen a long since discredited fashion and covered the walls with cladding tiles. Presumably the same person had built a porch in corrugated green plastic round the front door. It was the final insult to the house, which now looked totally charmless.

Stopping at the gate, they looked at each other and Sibylla shook her head sadly, to show what a lousy idea she thought it was. That decided Patrik, who at once started strolling along the garden path.

Sighing, she followed him. She couldn't just stand there, after all.

'What are you going to say?'

Before he had time to answer, a window was opened in the neighbouring house and a middle-aged woman popped her head out.

'Is it Gunvor you're looking for?'

They exchanged a quick glance.

'Yes,' they chorused.

'She's gone to the cottage. It's in Segersvik. Shall I tell her you called?'

Patrik went up to the hedge separating the two properties.

'Is it far to Segersvik?'

'Twenty-odd kilometres, I suppose. Are you driving?'

Patrik showed no hesitation.

'Yes, we are.'

'Right. Take the old road towards Gamleby, past Piperkärr and then carry on for another ten kilometres or so. I think there's a sign to Segersvik.'

'Thanks a lot.'

He turned, dispelling any other questions the woman might have wanted to ask. They walked down the path and heard her close the window. He spoke very quietly.

'That's where he was killed. The news stories say he was killed while staying in his summer cottage.'

They kept walking until they were outside the range of the woman next door. Sibylla stopped at the end of the street.

'Now what do we do? If we set out walking, we won't get back in time for the bus.'

'Sure. We'll take a taxi. I've got money.'

This sounded worrying.

'How come you've got such a lot? I mean, at your age one usually doesn't. Or have times changed?'

He said nothing, just kept his eyes fixed on the street.

'For fuck's sake, Patrik – you haven't nicked it, have you?'

'No, I haven't. Borrowed some, though.'

'Who lent you money?'

There was a taxi rank at the bus terminal and he started walking back. Sibylla didn't move.

'I won't take another step until you tell me where you got the money.'

'I borrowed some. Back home, from the household kitty. Relax, I'll pay it back before anyone notices.'

'Will you? With what, exactly?'

'I don't know. I mean, I'll think of something.'

He walked on but she still didn't move from the spot. Turning, he shouted irritably at her.

'What's wrong, do you just want to stand here bullshitting? Or what?'

'How much did you take?'

He hesitated.

'One grand.'

She took another sacred thousand-kronor note from her purse.

'Here, take it. And if you ever nick one single thing again, I'll leave. I mean it.'

He nodded, looking surprised.

'Do you get that?'

'*Yes*!'

He grabbed the note.

She set out for the bus station and when she turned her head, he was still standing there.

'Hey! What do you want, more bullshitting? Come on!'

He hesitated for another second and then, unwillingly, started running after her.

She was appalled when the meter clocked up more than two hundred kronor. Going places by taxi was grossly wasteful. Unheard of.

They had left Piperkärr far behind. The tarmac road had turned into a narrow gravel track through forest, now and then interrupted by farms and fields. The land was hilly, even rocky at times. They didn't speak. The driver luckily was a silent man and Patrik seemed to have withdrawn after being told off.

It made her feel better, because now she was back in charge.

Then they reached the lakeside. There was a small marina. The jetty was empty and the boats were hauled up on land, resting under tarpaulins and waiting for the spring. Afterwards, the road went through more forest until the landscape opened up towards the lake again. The sun was sinking, colouring the western sky an intense pink.

'Do you want the farm?'

The driver nodded his head in the direction of a group of buildings just ahead. Sibylla glanced at Patrik, who sat turned away and looking out through the window. He wasn't going to help, that much was clear. She leaned forward.

'I'm not really sure. We're visiting someone

called Gunvor Strömberg. She's staying in a cottage somewhere near here.'

The driver sounded sour.

'You've got to do better than that. Don't you have her address?'

He drove on slowly, past the gate of small red house on a sharp right-hand bend. The meter had clicked on to two hundred and sixty kronor. Sibylla swallowed and produced another note from her purse. Patrik glared at her but she avoided his eyes.

'We'll get off here.'

The taxi pulled in as far as possible on the narrow road. She paid but did not tip, so he made no move to help her lift her rucksack from the boot. The taxi turned at a meeting-place a bit further along and disappeared in the direction of town. It struck her that they hadn't planned the return journey. She sighed and heaved the rucksack onto her back.

The gate was open and the gap was wide enough to let a car through. There was a green tin letterbox with a name-tag. STRÖMBERG.

She turned towards Patrik.

'This is it. The cottage is by the water's edge.'

'Yeah.'

He sounded indifferent.

'How long are you going to sulk for?'

He didn't answer but walked along with her. The path leading to the house ran sharply downwards but after a short walk they could see the roof of a house. The rest of it was hidden behind tall shrubbery. Sibylla walked on, followed by Patrik. Once they got round the shrubbery the lake spread out in front of them. A jetty ran out into the water.

The view was stunningly beautiful. How could anyone be murdered in such a place as this?

'Are you looking for someone?'

Sibylla turned quickly. A woman was standing above them on the slope, next to a veranda on the lake side of the house. She had to think of something to say, because it was obvious that she was on her own now. Patrik was drifting off in the general direction of the jetty.

The woman, who could have been in her mid-sixties, had been tidying the lawn but she put the rake away. She was limping a little as she took a few steps to meet Sibylla. They met in silence and Sibylla could feel a pulse beating at her temple. What next?

'Have you come to look at the cottage? I'm afraid the estate agent didn't say.'

Of course! They were prospective buyers. Sibylla smiled gratefully.

'Yes, we are. If you don't mind?'

The woman smiled in response.

'I see. I'm sorry if I sounded a little cross, but . . . you see, lots of people came here just because they're . . . curious. Anyway, lucky I was here.'

She cleared her throat, pulled off her gardening gloves and held out her hand.

'Pleased to meet you. My name is Strömberg. Gunvor Strömberg.'

Sibylla took a fraction too long to answer.

'Sorry we were unexpected. I'm Margareta Lundgren.'

They shook hands. Gunvor Strömberg's hand was warm and a little damp after wearing the glove.

'Is that your son?'

They both looked towards Patrik's back. Sibylla laughed nervously.

'Absolutely. Yes.'

Patrik was throwing stones into the water. Sibylla's heart was beating too fast. He was so demonstratively unhelpful. How upset was he? Would he actually try to punish her?

'The jetty doesn't come with the house, but we do have the right of use. That's in the deeds. Actually, we use it more than anybody else.'

She fell silent, looking out over the water. Then she pulled herself together.

'I suppose you'd like to start indoors?'

Sibylla smiled.

'Please. Thank you.'

'What about the young man?'

Patrik was still throwing stones.

'Patrik, come along! We're going to look at the cottage.'

He didn't come at first. After throwing another stone, he started ambling back up from the jetty. Gunvor Strömberg smiled at Sibylla.

'Oh dear, it's such a difficult age, isn't it? I always felt that all you could do was let them get on with life on their own.'

Sibylla tried a smile of complicity. Damn his special age, whatever it was, she'd tell him a thing or two as soon as they were on their own.

Gunvor was walking ahead towards the house while Sibylla waited until Patrik joined her. When he was at whispering distance, she hissed at him.

'Get your fucking act together! She thinks we want to buy the place.'

He raised his eyebrows.

'Why don't you? You've got plenty stashed away, seemingly.'

He passed her on the path. This was the second time in one week that her money had angered and disappointed someone. Why did they take it out on her?

Gunvor was waiting for them and Sibylla hurried along. Meanwhile Patrik had introduced himself politely.

'Why don't you have a look around on your own? I'll be out here if you want me.'

After exchanging a quick glance, they climbed the stone steps to the front door.

'It's quite small but well equipped, I think you'll agree. The immersion heater is a little old though.'

Sibylla nodded and they stepped inside. The murderer must have come in this way once. After crossing a lobby, they were in a small kitchen. Everything was neat and well looked after. The atmosphere was cosy, familiar. Scruffy patches on the floor showed where kitchen chairs had been pulled up to and away from the table. The enamel on the handle on the oven door had been partly worn away after years of use by hungry hands.

There was a faint odour of paint in the air.

Patrik had gone on to open the door of a closed room. In the doorway, he stopped and signalled to her. She came to stand next to him. The room was unfurnished and freshly painted white. Patrik produced one of his pieces of paper. Pointing, he spoke in a whisper.

'That's the wall.'

Sibylla looked at the photograph of the blood-stained bed and read once more the killer's message, signed with her name. She wanted to get out, now.

Gunvor Strömberg had walked down to the jetty and stood there with her back to the house, staring out over the calm water of the lake. Sibylla felt she shouldn't disturb her. Patrik came alongside her.

'Go talk to her. I mean, it's not as if we've figured anything new yet. I'll stay here, just check it out a bit more.'

He was right. Of course they couldn't just leave now.

Gunvor Strömberg did not acknowledge Sibylla's presence in any way. Only when Sibylla cleared her throat noisily did her companion take her eyes away from the lake and raise a hand to wipe her face.

Still Gunvor did not turn round.

'It's a very nice place, this.'

No reply. For a while they stood together without speaking. Sibylla thought that sooner or later the silence would force the other woman to say something.

Looking at the wonderful view, Sibylla realised that this was the place she had always dreamt of. The quiet seclusion, the lovely natural setting. Not that she would ever be able to afford something like this. Besides, soon she wouldn't be able to buy anything at all. Suddenly Gunvor spoke, turning towards Sibylla.

'I suppose I'd better tell you myself, you'd only hear the rumours if I don't. You're not from round here, are you?'

'No, we're not.'

'I thought so.'

Sibylla took a few steps forward to stand

closer to the distressed woman. Silence was still her best policy.

'Six days ago, my husband was murdered in this house.'

Unobserved, Sibylla still acted out a silent reaction of surprise.

'The murderer wasn't local, if you're worrying about that.'

Sibylla had glimpsed enough of her face to see the tears flowing down Gunvor's cheeks.

'Is that why you want to sell your cottage?'

Gunvor sobbed, shaking her head at the same time.

'No, no. We'd planned to sell, but maybe in the spring when the prices are better.'

She sheltered her face behind her right hand, as if to hide her crying from Sibylla.

'Sören had been ill for quite a long time. Cancer of the liver. Just over a year ago he had major surgery and it went better than we dared hope. They gave him a forty-four per cent chance of surviving.'

She was shaking her head now.

'I suppose I'd started hoping again. He was taking his medicine and had regular check-ups. Things seemed all right. Well, he was often tired, no wonder, but he didn't like not being able to do what he used to. We thought keeping the cottage might become too much and, anyway, we could go travelling together with the money. After all, he mightn't . . . have that much time left.'

She stopped and Sibylla put her hand on Gunvor's shoulder. Gunvor started sobbing again when she felt the light touch.

'We spent as much time here as we could. Drove here the moment we were free.'

'Maybe you'd prefer not to sell immediately?'

Gunvor shook her head.

'I don't want to stay here any more. I don't like going into that house.'

Suddenly the silence was shattered by a flourish on a trumpet. Sibylla took her hand away and looked around in bewilderment.

'That Magnusson, a neighbour. When he's here, he plays reveille every morning and lights-out every night. It's from sheer joy at being here, he says.'

Gunvor had to smile a little, despite her grief. Sibylla closed her eyes, briefly dreaming of living in this place. Imagine having a neighbour, at a safe distance, who announced his presence with tunes on a trumpet, played from happiness. The dream of being happy.

'How much are you looking for? For the house?'

'The agent says I shouldn't go below 300,000 . . .'

Sibylla's hope went out like a light.

'. . . but as far as I'm concerned, what's important is who buys it.'

Their eyes met.

'Sören and I built it back in 1957, struggling

255

like anything to make ends meet. We've put so much of ourselves into this place, lived through so many things here. I still can't quite believe I can just move away. That the house will still be here, but with someone else inside it. Not us any more.'

She pulled her jacket closer around her body.

'As if we had never mattered.'

Sibylla protested, with real feeling.

'But you have mattered, of course you have. That's what makes it all so wonderful. The house bears witness to your lives here. The whole place does. Your feet made this path down to the lake and it will always be here. You planted the shrubs. Everything. I have never done anything that will live when I'm dead. Nothing to remind people that I was around.'

She stopped abruptly. What was all this in aid of? Why not give her name while she was at it?

'But you've got a son.'

Sibylla cleared her throat, embarrassed.

'Of course I do. I don't know what came over me.'

She turned to call.

'Patrik! I think we'd better go. We'll miss the bus!'

Gunvor looked concerned.

'Didn't you come by car?'

'No. We took a taxi here, actually.'

'I'll drive you to town. I'm leaving anyway.'

They made it to the bus terminal with only minutes to spare. Sibylla took a window seat. Clutched in her hand was a note with Gunvor Strömberg's telephone number, in case she decided to buy.

She put the note away in her pocket. Patrik was looking at her eagerly.

'Did you find out something?'

'I'm not sure. Probably not. She didn't say anything about the murder. He had cancer, badly. He had a big operation just a year or so ago.'

Patrik sounded disappointed.

'You should've asked about the murder.'

'Easier said than done.'

A moment later Patrik started examining his sheets of paper again. He had written something on the back of one them.

'What have you got there?'

'I copied a little from his hospital notes. Found them in a folder in her shoulder-bag.'

She was shocked.

'You rooted about in her bag?'

'Sure did. Do you want to find out stuff or not?'

A worse worry occurred to her.

'Hey, did you nick anything?'

'Yeah, of course. Stacks of cash.'

She made a face at him, reaching out her hand for his notes. He snatched back the sheet of paper.

'How come you're loaded?'

'What's your problem?'

'Why hang out in an attic when you're carrying umpteen grand in a purse round your neck?'

'That's my business.'

At first she didn't care if he started sulking again. He crossed his arms over his chest and turned away demonstratively. They were already driving into Söderköping when she finally admitted to herself that she owed him an explanation.

'It's my savings.'

He turned towards her.

Then she told him all of it, about her dream. The house that would open up a new life for her and about her mother's hand-outs, which had stopped when she hit the news.

He listened with interest. When she had finished, he held out his notes.

'There you are.'

He had been busy, copying lists of hospital stays and operations. She ignored the many incomprehensible expressions and abbreviations, until she was pulled up short by a word she had come across before. *Neoral*.

Someone had said that recently. Or had she read it? Patrik observed her reaction.

'What's up?'

She shook her head thoughtfully, pointing at it.

'I'm not sure. Here, look, where it says *Neoral*, fifty milligrams. I can't work out why I recognise this.'

'Seems to be some kind of medicine? Do you know what it's for?'

'Not a clue.'

'I know, Fiddie's mum is a doctor. I'll ask her.'

Brilliant. You just go ahead and ask Fiddie's mum why a patient should take *Neoral*. She must be used to teenagers asking her things like that on a daily basis. She smiled at him, wanting to take his hand. Better not.

'Patrik.'

'Ummm.'

'Thank you for everything, for your help.'

He seemed embarrassed.

'Oh, come on. I haven't helped any, not yet.'

Her smile grew broader.

'You really have.'

She spent the night in the attic of Patrik's block of flats. He let her in and she took up residence in an unused box-room. It had been hard for her to calm down. It was not hunger that kept her awake, because Patrik had brought her sandwiches. Her mind was stuffed with experiences and she needed to process them. Thoughts and images were flickering behind her eyelids. When she finally fell asleep she had been thinking for hours.

As soon as she woke up that Sunday morning, she knew why she had recognised *Neoral*. Her brain had sifted through stored information while she slept and it now presented her with the vital item.

Jörgen Grundberg. He had a packet of tablets and had taken some at the end of his meal. She sat bolt upright. This was surely important, it couldn't be a coincidence that two of the murderer's victims took the same medicine?

She felt wide-awake and had to walk about. Impatiently she went into the corridor outside to peer through the only small window. It was light outside and she wondered what time it was. How long before Patrik would come?

She had to wait for hours. While she waited, the effect of this sudden breakthrough became clear to her. Once more, the will to fight was consuming her.

When she finally heard the heavy metal door swing open and Patrik called her name, she couldn't wait a second longer to tell him.

'Jörgen Grundberg took *Neoral* as well!'

'Did he? Are you sure?'

He gave her a triple-decker sandwich and a beer, but she was too excited to eat.

'Certain. It can't be coincidence, can it?'

'I asked Fiddie's mum.'

'Already? What time is it?'

'Ten past eleven. I phoned her. Woke her up, actually. I said I was doing this Special Subject investigation. No lies!'

He grinned.

'I had chased it on the Net first, but couldn't get my head round what it was for.'

'And?'

He pulled a piece of paper from his pocket.

'It's called an immunosuppressive drug. If you're on it, it means you've had a transplant. The medicine prevents the new organ being rejected by the person's body cells.'

He looked triumphant when he put his paper away.

'Transplant – like a new organ? A heart or something?'

'That's it. She said there are lots of bits and pieces you replace in people's bodies.'

Sibylla sat down to think. First, Jörgen Grundberg. He had had a kidney disease, or so his hard-hearted widow had told her. Sören Strömberg's widow had told her about his liver cancer. Both were on medicine that reduced the function of their immune systems. Both widows had mentioned that their husbands had undergone major surgery within the last year.

This could not be coincidental.

'Are you thinking the same as me?'

Sibylla nodded.

'As I. Yes, I'm sure I am. If we can, we should check it out at least once more. Do you have that list?'

He nodded.

'Downstairs. Hang on, I'll get it.'

When he returned, he'd also brought his father's mobile phone. She read the by now familiar names once more.

'What next? Which one do you want to call? Bollnäs or Stocksund?'

Put like that, she suddenly didn't think it was such a good idea. She would have preferred him to call, but it meant ceding control and that was something she definitely didn't want to do. He had got her going again and she was truly grateful, but she wanted to continue under her own steam.

'I'll call Stocksund.'

'Good. Here's the number, I checked it out in the book.'

He helped her dial. At first, the phone rang without anyone answering. Patrik kept watching her and her heart was pounding. It would have been easier alone. She was not used to lying in front of an audience.

'Mårten Samuelsson.'

The sudden sound of a voice at the other end threw her. The many signals had distracted her.

'I'm sorry to trouble you. Is this Sofie Samuelsson's husband?'

Fantastic introduction. She closed her eyes. Whoever he was, for sure he wasn't Sofie Samuelsson's husband. Not any more.

'Who's speaking, please?'

She looked around, as if useful answers might be lurking in attic corners.

'This is . . .'

Patrik was miming *the police*.

'. . . from the police.'

Silence at the other end.

'Just one question. Did your wife have an organ transplant recently?'

'I told you so already.'

She nodded to Patrik. He rolled his eyes.

'When was this?'

'Whenever you people came round here.'

'No, I mean the operation.'

'Thirteen months ago.'

'I see. Can you remember the date?'

'The fifteenth of March. I'll never forget that date. Why do you ask?'

'No problem. Thank you for your help.'

She handed Patrik the phone. He pressed a button to switch it off and sighed.

'Why don't you try the straight question approach next time?'

'You can phone yourself if you're so smart. When was Sören Strömberg operated on?'

Patrik was leafing through his papers looking for the hospital notes.

'Many times.'

'Any entry on the fifteenth of March?'

'Got it. 98 03 15. Liver transplant.'

She nodded. He pushed his fist in the air.

'*Yees!* We fucking did it!'

Sibylla felt pleased, too, but was already thinking ahead. What had they proved, exactly? It seemed likely that all four victims were ex-transplant patients. What did this mean? Why should anyone go to the trouble of murdering four severely ill individuals?

Patrik's eyes were glowing behind his specs.

'I'll pop downstairs and tell Mum!'

'What? Have you gone off your . . .'

'Why not? We've got a motive!'

'Is that so? What motive?'

Patrik fell silent and a small vertical fold between his eyebrows replaced his smile.

'Oh. Fuck.'

'See what I mean?'

He sat down beside her. The attic was chilly and Sibylla wrapped the sleeping bag round their shoulders.

'Is your Mum back then?'

She was reaching for the beer and sandwich.

'I thought you said she wouldn't be back until this evening.'

Patrik stared at the floor. He was muttering. 'She didn't feel well and came back early.'

T he minutes were crawling along. He had asked her to come with him but she'd refused. She had no intention of entering his home again, especially not with his mother in bed next door to his room.

Finally he returned, bringing a new stack of papers. He sat down beside her.

'I printed out lots, but ran out of paper. Fancy a banana?'

Starting to peel it at once, she thought she was becoming spoiled by this life of luxury. Then she got hold of the first sheet of paper.

DONATIONS. ANSWERS TO THE MOST FRE-QUENTLY ASKED QUESTIONS.

Deep in concentration, they read through all the information in the pile, hoping to find new leads. Patrik was lying on her mat, while she was sitting in an old armchair pulled out from an unlocked box-room.

CAN SOMEONE ELSE USE YOUR KIDNEYS AFTER YOUR DEATH?

Reading on from this initial question, she realised that much had happened while she was out of touch with the whole social system. She definitely had not filled in any Donor Card, but maybe that didn't affect non-people like herself. What would happen to her after an accident? Would anyone want her remains? She had never considered such questions before, not even the matter of her final burial. Were there funeral services held for lost souls like her, homeless beings, whom no one really cared for? Maybe they were easy meat, with organs anyone could have, if in need of some replacement or other. Well, it was quite a thought that one day she might be regarded as a useful resource.

LAW ON TRANSPLANTATION, THIRD PARAGRAPH, SECTION ONE:

Biological material intended for transplantation or other medical procedures may be removed from a deceased person, on condition that the person has declared his or her informed consent or if the deceased's wishes in the matter can be ascertained in any other manner.

Biological material, as simple as that. That's what they all were, when everything was said and done. She wondered what conclusions they would draw about Sibylla Forsenström's wishes in the matter of her biological material, when her day finally came.

In cases other than those indicated in section one, biological material may be removed if the deceased has not in writing declared him- or herself explicitly opposed to such use or made declarations, which unequivocally show that such interventions would be contrary to the deceased's beliefs or value-systems.

She looked up from her bundle of paper and stared at the wooden planks in the wall opposite. So that was it – it was open season to use her and her mates. One man's meat is another man's poison, only the other way round. What would it feel like to have another's heart, especially if it was kept alive and beating only when you took medicines to stop your familiar old body from ridding itself of its heart? And the nearest and dearest, what did they feel? What was it like, knowing that your beloved's heart was still there, inside someone else?

Patrik's voice interrupted her musings.

'Found anything?'

'Not really. Have you?'

Since he didn't answer, she assumed he hadn't, and returned to her reading.

Even if biological material can be removed as described in Paragraph three, section two, such procedures are not permitted in cases where someone close to the deceased is strongly opposed to the intervention. Close relations by blood or marriage must be informed about the planned intervention and about their right to forbid it. After such information has been provided, the informed must be allowed a reasonable period of time to consider it.

She read it all through once more. Then she put the paper down and rose, slowly turning the idea over in her mind. It was right, she could feel it all over.

ACCURSED ARE THOSE WHO ROB THE INNOCENTS OF THEIR RIGHTS.

'Patrik!'

'Ummm.'

'I've got it!'

She heard him shuffling behind the wooden partition and the next moment he was with her.

'What? How can you be sure?'

She was sure.

'The killer, it's someone who is regretting giving permission.'

Regret was what she had not been given a chance to do once.

ACCURSED ARE THOSE WHO ROB THE INNOCENTS OF THEIR RIGHTS.

The right to live. Or to die.

'It could be someone who wasn't asked at all.'

Patrik went back downstairs to commune with his computer. Meanwhile, she was impatiently pacing the corridor to pass the time.

The donor must have died just before 15 March, 1998. How could they find out who he or she was? Maybe there were lists of donors in that secret world Patrik could access through his computer. If there were, she felt certain he would find it. Everything seemed to be connected by that strange Net of his.

He mustn't say anything to his mother. She had forbidden him, deciding that she preferred to stay chief suspect for however long it took to find the answer alone. The police might be on the same trail – but why would they be? They knew who the murderer was already.

When Patrik returned, he had no good news to bring. There were no officially available registers of dead individuals, only general mortality statistics. It was not helpful to know that during the year, 93,271 people had died.

'I've checked the sites of the Population

Register and the Central Statistical Bureau, but they won't let you in on the actual lists without permission from the Data Inspection Office.'

He looked so young in his dejection that Sibylla had to smile.

'You've got to be an exceptionally smart fifteen-year-old!'

He turned his head away but she had already noticed how he blushed.

'Bah.'

They sat in silence for a while. Chasing murderers from hiding places in attics wasn't easy. Then Sibylla remembered something.

'I've got it. What we need is access to the Donor Register.'

'What's that?'

She knew more than he did this time and the feeling made her smile inside, even though her superior knowledge was very recent. She wasn't as thick as he might have thought, no poor helpless soul he could save by his bravery. Besides, she was twice his age and she wanted him never to forget that simple fact.

She fetched the pile of papers from her armchair, leafing through them until she found what she was looking for.

'Here, in the documentation from the Health and Welfare Board. Information about donations. Listen to what it says.'

She read aloud.

'*Question: Can relatives have access to information held in the register?*

Answer: It is a criminal offence for outsiders to attempt access to the register. The routine precautions are designed to maintain the highest data security. Only a few people are authorised to search the register. Each authorisation refers to one individual, i.e. it is not transferable.'

She flicked the paper out of her hand and let it float away.

'Ah, well. It seemed a good idea at the time.'

He looked intently at her.

'How much is it worth to you to find out what the Register says?'

'A lot.'

'Several thousand?'

She hesitated for a moment. Several thousand might mean half a bedroom.

'What's this about?'

'I know a guy who might check it out. For a down-payment, a big one.'

'How do you know people like that?'

'I don't, but his brother goes to my school. The kid brother is like royalty after the big guy served time for hacking data.'

This was not easy. However much she wanted the information, she wanted even less to risk having Patrik involved in breaking the law.

'How old is "the big guy"?'

Patrik shrugged.

'Don't know. Like, twenty?'

She thought it over. This was their one chance to move on. They had come so far already. She sighed.

'You're on. He gets three thousand for the name.'

S he had decided to go there herself. It was her problem and, besides, she definitely didn't want Patrik to get involved in this shady affair. He had helped enough by anonymously arranging the deal using his father's mobile phone. The price had been agreed. Four thousand kronor.

Sibylla touched the purse round her neck, feeling its shrinking bulge. It was hard, but what choice did she have?

Patrik had asked why she was hauling the rucksack along, and was told the simple reason. She never left it anywhere, except in the Left Luggage at Central Station. It meant she had security in the shape of a locker key or a receipt.

The master hacker lived on Kock Street, only a few minutes' walk away. Patrik stopped outside the door and pressed the buzzer. The door clicked open at once.

'Are you waiting round here?'

He was still disappointed that she wouldn't let him join her.

'Patrik, this is the best idea – honestly.'

The door slammed behind her. She walked upstairs to the second floor, where a young man with sleek blond hair stood waiting at the door to a flat. Sibylla stopped and they examined each other in silence.

After a few seconds of this, he opened the door wide for her. He was wearing a white T-shirt, revealing muscular arms with prominent veins. He must have worked out hard in prison. As he walked ahead of her into the flat, she noticed that his hair had been pulled back in a long pony-tail.

The flat was small, just a single room with a kitchenette. The sink was so full of dishes she wondered if he ever washed up. There was a rack with a set of dumb-bells in a corner. Next to it, a yellow electric guitar was leaning against its amplifier. A long window wall was entirely taken up by computer equipment and other electronic goods she couldn't even guess the function of. Presumably, this was the kind of kit self-respecting hackers simply couldn't live without. Two of the screens showed a series of letters and numbers scrolling past quickly. She moved towards them to see what was going on.

He stepped into her path.

'Not so fast. It's practically ready. Let's do the paying first, shall we?'

She was clutching the notes in her pocket.

'No problem.'

He took the bundle without checking it.

'Sit down over there.'

He was pointing to a stool well away from the computers, in fact almost inside the small hallway. She did as she was told, keeping her rucksack on her back but resting it a little against the wall behind her.

She couldn't see much from where she was sitting, but by leaning forward it was possible to watch him working on one of the computers. He was writing things using the keyboard and his fingers were moving at an incredible speed. She marvelled at his skill and wondered how his huge hands could work with such precision.

'You're in luck.'

He was muttering, not taking his eyes off the screen.

'Someone went in for a search just now, so all we need to do is hang on.'

He stopped keying and she sat upright again, looking at the wall. She didn't want to be caught out spying on him.

Would he recognise any of the names from the newspapers? Jörgen Grundberg's name had been used a lot, almost as often as her own.

When she heard him get up from the chair, she rose too. Then he come over, holding out one folded sheet of A4 paper.

'Done.'

She took the paper without taking her eyes off his face.

'You're sure it's the right person?'

He smiled, clearly never having heard such a stupid question before.

'Yes, don't worry.'

He sounded soothing.

'Depends, of course. But he's the guy whose organs were transplanted into the names on your list.'

He looked quizzically at her.

'Weren't they all murdered afterwards? By some character called Sibylla?'

She didn't answer. He smiled broadly.

'Just so that we know where we are, you know.'

She put the paper in her pocket, unafraid because he couldn't threaten to reveal her identity. If one of them talked, the other one would and they shared that knowledge.

She looked at him, reflecting on how his big muscles seemed matched by his brain. Just as she put her hand on the door handle to leave, another thought occurred to her.

'Haven't you ever thought of getting a real job? You have all the qualifications for a good one, it seems.'

He was leaning against the door frame to the main room, his bulging arms crossed over his chest. He was grinning openly at her now.

'No, I haven't. Have you?'

Then she left.

Thomas Sandberg. That was all it said on the note she showed Patrik. They were standing together in the street, reading the name over and over again, as if reading a long story rather than a sequence of fourteen letters.

'No address?'

'No.'

He looked disappointed. Obviously, he felt this was a poor show after an outlay of four thousand kronor.

'How many Thomas Sandbergs do you think there are in this country?'

She raised her eyebrows.

'No idea. All we do know is that there's one less now. Let's go.'

She started walking. She felt certain that what she was about to do next was the right thing, but even so she was troubled by the distance she would callously create between them. If she kept walking she wouldn't have to look into his eyes, which would make it a little easier.

'Now what do we do?'

He had hurried to catch up with her.

That instant the alarm in his wristwatch went off.

'Christ! Sunday lunch!'

He turned off the signal.

'Mum forced me to set the alarm. She'll have a fit if I don't turn up.'

'Don't risk it. Off you go.'

'Do you want to keep hanging out in the attic?'

She didn't reply.

'Do you?'

'Maybe that's the best idea.'

She hadn't even lied. It almost certainly was the best idea if she stayed hidden in Patrik's attic for the foreseeable future, allowing him to feed her the leftovers from the family meals.

Be that as it may. It was too late now.

Somewhere, a man or a woman existed, who had had an improbable stroke of luck when their paths crossed that night in the Grand Hotel. That person had stolen her name and exploited her outsider's isolation to further a purely personal vendetta.

She was not going to let that pass. The invisible one had almost succeeded in crushing her. Almost, but not quite.

When the large iron door leading to Patrik's attic had slammed behind her and Patrik's steps were disappearing down the stairs, she pulled the second sheet of A4 paper from her pocket.

She read it carefully, memorising the text.

Rune Hedlund. ID 46 06 08 – 2498 res. Vimmerby.

The cemetery was large and it took her the best part of an hour to find the tombstone. It was tucked away in the parkland set aside for urns, a rounded natural boulder with an inscription in gold lettering.

RUNE HEDLUND
* 8 JUNE 1946
† 15 MARCH 1998

Below was a space large enough for another name. An eternal flame was burning inside a white plastic cover. Yellow and purple crocuses were filling the area round the stone. Spring arrived earlier this far south.

She crouched down. Noticing some dry leaves caught between the spring flowers, she pulled them out and threw them to the wind.

'What are you doing here?'

The voice behind her startled her so much she lost her balance and sat down with a thump. She rose quickly, turning to look at the woman who had crept up behind her. Sibylla's heart was racing.

'Just removing some dead leaves.'

Their eyes met, fiercely, as if facing each other across a battle demarcation line. The woman's eyes were full of suspicion and dislike. Sibylla suddenly felt sure she had found her quarry.

They faced up to each other in hostile silence. Sibylla's adversary was dressed in white under her grey coat and she had brought along a green, funnel-shaped vase filled with multi-coloured tulips.

'You're not to mess about with my husband's grave.'

Aha. Rune Hedlund's widow.

'I was just clearing some leaves away.'

The woman breathed heavily through her nose, as if trying to pull herself together.

'What have you got to do with my husband?'

'I never met him.'

The woman smiled suddenly, but there was no friendliness in her smile. Fear started creeping up on Sibylla. Had the woman recognised her? The police might have worked out the link between the killings and the organ transplant and asked Hedlund's wife to keep a look-out for Sibylla. They would be keen to find a link between them, to trace Sibylla's motive.

She glanced over her shoulder. Maybe they were here already?

'Don't you realise I know what you've been up to for ages?'

After a pause the woman spoke again.

'I knew ever since the funeral, when I saw your flowers.'

She sounded outraged.

'What's going on in the mind of someone sending an anonymous bouquet of red roses to a funeral? What did you hope to gain by it? Can you tell me that? Did you think it would please Rune?'

The contempt in the woman's eyes was so searing that Sibylla had to look away.

'If he really wanted to live with you he'd have chosen you while he was alive. But he stayed with me. Not you. So was that why you had to produce the flowers – to humiliate me?'

The woman frowned demonstratively as if she was trying to make the revulsion she felt visible.

'Every Friday, week in and week out, one more bloody red rose on his grave. Do you want to punish me? Make me suffer because I was the one who got him in the end?'

Her voice was cracking, but it was obvious that she had stored up more to say. Words had been piling up, waiting for an outlet.

Sibylla was shaken by her own miscalculation. The authorities would have had to ask this woman. She was one of the 'close relatives' whose informed consent must be sought.

The answer was presumably that someone else out there was feeling abandoned and bitterly wanted to restore something of what had been lost. She had to make sure.

'Have the police contacted you?'

'What? The police? Why should they?'

Rune Hedlund's widow took a step forward, kneeled and jammed the sharp tip of her tin vase into the ground. The crocuses shied away in alarm.

Watching the other woman's back rising and falling with her heavy breathing, Sibylla was quite sure that she had been looking forward to this moment of confrontation. She had probably practised carefully what to say when she was finally face to face with her husband's unknown mistress.

Shame that she had wasted her ammunition.

Of course, she was not to know that Rune's real lover had committed much, much worse acts than putting flowers on her man's grave. Sibylla wouldn't like to be the one who enlightened her.

When the distraught woman got up, there were tears in her eyes.

'You're sick – you realise that, don't you?'

The detestation in her eyes hit Sibylla almost like a physical blow. Old memories came back and she looked away to stop remembering.

'Can't let him be, can you? Not even in death?'

She walked away. Sibylla just stood there, watching her disappear.

It was obvious that Rune Hedlund's widow had no idea of how right she was, in a way.

S he stayed in the cemetery, sitting on a bench she had picked for its good view of Rune Hedlund's final resting place, even though it was a safe distance away. Not many people had decided to visit their loved ones' graves that day and those who did come were either couples or too old.

Not that she was in a hurry. She was ready to stay until that woman came. Sooner or later she would.

At nightfall she pulled out her sleeping bag and mat. There was a stone wall at the back of the urn enclosure and she tucked herself up between it and the bare branches of shrubbery. It was reasonably out of sight, but it also allowed her to keep watch at all times. Not that she thought the woman would turn up this late, but from what she had learned about her she was well able to surprise.

She wouldn't miss this woman when she finally came.

*   *   *

The next day she picked another bench to sit on. It was less well placed for observing the grave, but the wife's big bouquet of tulips helped by marking it out. She left her station only once, when she ran to the nearby garage to use their toilet and buy bread. It took only ten minutes before she was back in place, resuming her guard.

No one came near Rune Hedlund's grave.

The next day she fell asleep. She did not know for how long but rushed to the grave to check. No red rose had turned up during the night.

On the Wednesday she felt her pulse beat faster, for the first time. A solitary woman in her forties turned the corner by the water tap and walked briskly along the path towards the urn enclosure.

Sibylla hurried away, taking a shortcut across a small lawn to keep an eye on what was happening. The woman disappointed her by continuing past the pink and yellow tulips to bend over a stone a little further along.

Sibylla returned to her bench with a sigh.

By that afternoon she was feeling real hunger pangs. Taking money from her savings had almost become a habit and it didn't bother her any more. With a last look at the deserted cemetery, she went off to the handy garage. She used the toilet again, just in case, and bought two grilled hot dogs with plenty of mustard and ketchup.

When she returned, a man wearing a brown suede jacket was crouching in front of Rune Hedlund's grave. The hair on the back of his head was thinning.

It might be awkward, but she couldn't afford to pass up this opportunity. She had been watching round the clock for days to find out more and, whoever he was, he must have known Rune Hedlund well. He was bending deep over the grave in prayer or contemplation. Shoving the last piece of sausage into her mouth, she walked closer, all the time chewing and swallowing carefully. In passing, she grabbed a fresh-looking bunch of daffodils from a nearby grave. Necessity knows no law.

Hopefully, the spirit of Sigfrid Stålberg wouldn't mind too much.

She stopped just behind the man, who had shifted position and was sitting on his haunches by the grave, just as she had a couple of days ago. He was fiddling intently with something near the tombstone and seemed not to have heard her. She couldn't see what he was up to. Watching him made her suddenly feel very ill at ease. If she was to gain his confidence, sneaking up on him like this was hardly the way to go about it.

She cleared her throat.

His reaction was rather similar to her own earlier. He momentarily lost his balance, but steadied himself by leaning on one hand. She smiled apologetically.

'I'm sorry I startled you.'

He was younger-looking than she had expected. Recovering quickly from his confusion, he turned his face up and smiled back at her.

'You're a right menace, creeping up on people like that. I might've had a heart attack.'

'Honestly, I didn't mean to. It's the soles on my shoes.'

He looked at her sturdy, comfy walking boots. Then his gaze wandered to her face. He sniffled a little, wiping his nose with his hand. Then he looked at the grave.

'Are you here for Rune?'

Damn it! He had got his question in first and that was bad.

She moved her head about in a way that could have signified either a reluctant Yes or a muddled No, whatever the circumstances called for.

'Did you know him?'

She got her question in quickly, trying to take over control.

He looked her over, neither suspiciously nor unpleasantly, but with interest. Apparently, he was feeling genuinely curious about her. Then he shook his head a little.

'Know and know. We were workmates, down in Åbro village.'

'I see.'

'And you, what about you? Are you a relative?'

'Oh no.'

Her answer had sounded far too pat. He smiled a little.

'Now you've really made me curious. I'm sure you're not from round here.'

She shook her head and looked down. The daffodils caught her eyes. She would get a little respite if she fetched a vase and some water.

'Hey, I'd better look after these.'

Without giving him a chance to say any more, she walked across to the small fenced-in maintenance area. He was quick – fast on the draw and inquisitive. She realised she couldn't get rid of him without telling him who she was.

So, who was she?

She took her time. She picked a sharp-tipped plastic vase from the box and rinsed it carefully under running water. Fragmented thoughts were rotating wildly in her brain, as if spun in a centrifuge. How to avoid raising his suspicions? Why had she approached him anyway?

With the vase filled for the fourth time, she walked back. She drew a deep breath. He was crouching near the grave again and pushed apart the stems in a clump of crocuses. There were paint-stains on his hands.

The fingers were long and slender. He wore no rings.

'Why don't you put your flowers here?'

She followed his advice. A crocus flipped forward and she pushed it back. He reached out and put his finger on her watch.

'What an unusual watch.'

She felt a little silly and pulled her sleeve down to cover the watch.

'It's old. It doesn't even work any more.'

She glanced sideways at him. His eyes were suddenly fixed on the tombstone.

'Ingmar!'

This time they both practically fell over backwards.

'What are you doing here? And with her!'

Mrs Hedlund was making no bones about it – she didn't care at all for the scene at her husband's grave. Her voice held surprise, but also anger and suspicion.

'Kerstin – please!'

The man called Ingmar took a step towards the agitated woman.

'I'm not here "with her". I thought she was a friend of the family.'

He was at Kerstin Hedlund's side, looking at Sibylla. His move over to the right team had been fast. Sibylla was left with the guilt, one foot still planted among the crocuses. Kerstin was staring at her now, her eyes brimming with an emotion that was composed of grief and hatred. At the same time, her face expressed such condescension that Sibylla felt ready to apologise for just existing.

Ingmar turned his head from one woman to the other. Finally his curiosity won.

'Who is she?'

He was clearly struggling to keep his voice neutral. Kerstin Hedlund answered, her eyes pinning Sibylla to the spot.

'She's nobody. I'd be grateful if you got her out of here. At once.'

He looked at Sibylla, who nodded quickly and stepped across to the path. Anything to end this performance.

'Hurry up, and come with me!'

He made an impatient gesture. Sibylla obeyed immediately, but gave the furious woman a wide berth. Mustn't get involved in anything noisy.

Neither of them spoke before reaching the parking lot. Her rucksack was still hidden in the shrubbery, but there was no way she could fetch it now. She had to come back later, somehow.

He turned to her.

'What was all that in aid of?'

Knowing that evasiveness was pointless, Sibylla hesitated just a fraction of a second.

'She thinks I'm Rune's mistress.'

He laughed abruptly. Maybe she ought to take offence.

'She's convinced he had one, because somebody is putting a red rose on his grave every week.'

His smile faded and was replaced by a frown. He sighed deeply.

'Do you know Kerstin?'

'No.'

He glanced at the cemetery, as if to reassure himself that they had not been followed.

'I understand that you felt very uncomfortable, but you must try to forgive her.'

'Forgive her – I don't understand what you mean.'

He sighed again. It seemed to distress him to speak ill of the widow.

'You see, it's Kerstin herself who puts roses on the grave. She forgets it afterwards and goes around accusing people she meets in the cemetery. She's been very distraught and unlike her usual self, ever since Rune died.'

Sibylla stared at him. He sensed her confusion and went on with his explanation before she got round to asking more questions.

'I came here today in a reflective mood. I don't know what I can do to help her, but I feel I owe Rune the effort.'

Sibylla still didn't get it. If there was no mistress, then . . . the next conclusion was inevitable.

'In what way hasn't she been her usual self?'

He looked downcast and embarrassed.

'She's been off work for a couple of months now. She was employed at the Health Centre as a practice nurse, but they felt she was behaving irrationally and told her to take some time off. Sadly, she seems to have gone from bad to worse since she stopped working.'

Sibylla recalled the white clothes under Kerstin Hedlund's coat when they first met.

'But I'm sure I've seen her in her uniform.'

He nodded sadly.

'Yes. I know, I know.'

So, her instinctive reaction had been right. She was the one, that woman with hate in her eyes. The healthcare job would mean easier access to the transplant lists. Having traced the victims, all she did was to find them and bring back what she reckoned was justly hers.

That Sibylla Forsenström's life was crushed in the process was obviously of zero importance. Well, in some ways it had actually been an encouraging coincidence, which could be put to good use. She closed her eyes to hide the fury in them. The desire to hurt that woman, badly enough to mark her for life, invaded Sibylla's whole body. So much anguish, so many anxious moments – and above all, the loss of her savings and her hopes of a better future. She turned and walked towards the cemetery gates.

He called after her.

'Where are you off to?'

Sibylla didn't answer.

Looking around the cemetery she realised that it was empty. Kerstin Hedlund must have left by another gate. She rejoined Ingmar.

'Where does Kerstin live?'

He looked concerned.

'Why do you ask?'

'I'd like to speak to her for a while.'

By now his voice was carrying a distinct note of caution.

'Is that really wise?'

She raised her eyebrows. Wise? Well, for a start it wasn't Sibylla who had laid down the rules. Maybe the determination showed in her face and manner, for he made no further attempts to dissuade her, only sighed, as if he regretted being involved at all.

'I'll drive you. It's too far to walk.'

S he forgot about her rucksack, for her mind was entirely dominated by the thought of revenge and punishment. Ingmar drove his old Volvo in silence through Vimmerby town centre, past blocks of flats and then a housing estate. When they had left the built-up areas behind, the road went through woodland.

Sibylla wasn't watching.

'Accursed is he who deprives the innocent of his rights.'

The words echoed in her mind, sounding like a premonition.

She didn't even notice at first that the car had stopped.

'It seems she isn't back home yet. At least, the car isn't here.'

His voice got through to her and took her away from her obsessional thoughts. Finding herself back in the passenger seat of the Volvo she looked outside. They had pulled up in front of a yellow wooden house. All the windows were covered by lowered Venetian blinds.

'I'll wait.'

She fumbled with the door handle to get out.

'It's raining.'

That was true enough. Water was rippling down the windscreen.

'I'm a neighbour. I live in the house over there. Why don't you come in for a cup of coffee while you're waiting?'

Coffee? She couldn't care less just now. On the other hand, saying no to anything nutritious was a bad idea and the hot dogs had done little to fill her up. There was plenty of space left inside. She nodded. He got into gear and the car crawled along between the gateposts of a roughcast, green-painted house opposite the Hedlund's.

So, they weren't next-door neighbours, but lived really near each other. Sibylla stepped out into the rain and waited for Ingmar. He walked up a gravelled path towards his house. When she stood on top of the steps, she turned to look, in case Kerstin Hedlund's car was coming down the road. All seemed quiet. He reassured her.

'You'll hear her when she comes. We're the only ones living out here.'

She stepped into the hall. A strong smell of solvents was hanging in the air.

'Damn, I forgot to take the jar of turps away.'

He disappeared out of sight but returned

quickly, carrying a glass jar with paint-brushes left in to soak.

'The smell will clear away soon. I'll just put the jar outside for now.'

He opened the front door, put the offending jar outside, closed the door and turned the key in the lock. She found a spare hook and hung up her jacket.

'Do you paint?'

'It's just a hobby of mine. Why don't you come into the kitchen? We might as well have a cup of coffee.'

He bent to take off his shoes and she followed his example. He stood back to let her step into the kitchen first.

As she took it in she felt sure that this man wasn't living alone. The place wasn't just clean and tidy, but nicely looked after. There were white lace curtains in the window, drawn back by neat, pale pink ties. There were several pots of healthy-looking and quite unusual plants on the windowsill, which was protected by a crocheted runner, possibly home-made.

He was fiddling with the coffee things, filling the kettle with water.

'Why don't you sit down – make yourself at home?'

She found a chair that allowed her to keep watch on the road. He was measuring the coffee from a pretty but worn tin. Observing him as he was pottering about, she thought that there was something odd about the place. Everything was cared for and in good order, but curiously old-fashioned. The kitchen furnishings looked like 1950s' originals and the workbenches were far too low, barely reaching the tops of his thighs. Whoever lived here certainly had no interest in up-to-date interior decorating. Still, who was she to criticise?

'Do you live here alone?'

He looked at her. His expression was almost shy.

'Yes. I've been staying here on my own ever since my mother died.'

'I'm sorry. Did she die recently?'

The coffee-maker started bubbling.

'No, not at all. About ten years ago.'

But you still use her curtains, though.

'Would you like a sandwich?'

'Please. I'm quite hungry.'

He opened the fridge door. The handle was black Bakelite and the whole model looked ancient. Gun-Britt had had one of them in her flat in Hultaryd, thirty-five or so years ago. He hesitated, his hand still on the door handle.

'Oh no – what a shame. I've forgotten about the shopping. I'm afraid you'll have to be content with just coffee, after all.'

'No problem.'

He opened one of the kitchen cabinets, taking out pretty cups and saucers with a blue flower pattern. He put them on the table and started rummaging in a drawer to find the coffee spoons. A car drove past on the road. She jumped and looked out, but the car drove past at speed, disappearing beyond the next bend in the road.

By now, Ingmar was folding napkins, delicate little squares of thin cloth with scalloped edges. She hadn't seen their like since the ladies' after-noon tea-parties in Hultaryd. Maybe this was to be expected in the countryside, where time moved so much more slowly than in towns.

'Only the best for visitors.'

She looked at him. He was busy, carefully smoothing the folds in the spotless waxed cloth covering the table. Getting the napkins from a drawer in the table had disturbed it. He was looking very pleased with himself, almost elated. Could it be that it was a long time since he experienced anything as convivial as having a guest for coffee? A female guest to boot.

Before pouring the coffee, he found a small silver tray in a cupboard. On it he placed a sugar-bowl and a cream jug in the same china as the cups. Looking very pleased with his preparations, he sat down opposite her and smiled invitingly.

'There now. Hope you'll enjoy it.'

'Thank you.'

She glanced at the empty cream jug. It would have been nice with a little milk out of a packet, but she realised that it was pointless to ask.

Lifting the cup by its tiny fragile handle, she drank some coffee while considering the text on the embroidered sampler behind him.

GREATEST OF ALL IS LOVE.

Then he suddenly broke the silence.

'So what's your plan for when you meet Kerstin?'

The question threw her. During the car journey her thoughts had been so intense that she had somehow assumed that he would share her sense of urgency. Now it struck her that he still had no idea who she was. She looked into her coffee cup.

'I just wanted to talk to her a little.'

The expression on his face didn't change, as if the smile had been glued to his face.

'Why do you?'

She felt something like irritation creeping into her mind. So maybe he meant well, but she wasn't that dependent on his good offices.

'It's something between her and me.'

Ingmar kept focusing on her.

'Are you sure?'

The coffee was thin and tasteless. He had put in far too little coffee. She had no energy left for maintaining this conversation and rose from the table.

'Thanks for the coffee and the lift. I feel like taking a little walk now, while I wait.'

He didn't answer and the smile still didn't leave his face. It suddenly came to her that there was something not quite right about him. His incessant smiling was so silly that she had an impulse to say something nasty, just to wipe it off his mug. He looked pleased with himself, as if remembering a funny story he had no intention of sharing with her.

She walked into the hall and started putting on her boots. When she straightened up and reached for her jacket he was standing in the kitchen doorway, positively grinning at her.

'You're not leaving already?'

His tone of voice made it sound more like an order than a question. This was the end of good manners, as far as she was concerned.

'Yes, I am. I can't stand coffee without milk, you see.'

'Is that so? I got the impression you weren't that picky.'

He had bitten suddenly, like a snake. Unhesitatingly ready to drop any attempt at choosing his word with care. She suddenly felt deeply uneasy. Taking down her jacket, at first she could think of nothing to say at all.

'What do you mean?'

When she finally spoke, she no longer felt quite so sure of herself and her voice must have revealed it, for the smile came back to his face.

'That's obvious, isn't it? People like you should be grateful for what they can get.'

She tried as best she could not to show how

frightened she was by now. He didn't look particularly strong, but that was a miscalculation
she had made before and duly suffered for. If
they were hungry enough for what they wanted,
she had rarely had a chance. No way was she
giving in without a fight, though. She backed
away from him.

'Vimmerby seems to be one hell of a place. A
serial killer and a rapist living just next door to
each other. Maybe there's something nasty in
the water?'

She glanced towards the front door. The key
had gone.

'It's locked, in case you wondered.'

He had an informative tone to his voice.

'Now, there's something else I should let you
know. If there's one thing I haven't got the
slightest inclination to do, it's keeping you here
for sex.'

This did nothing to convince her. She backed
away from him, hitting her back against the end
of the stair railing.

'There are other things we've got to sort out
together, you and I.'

She swallowed.

'I don't think so.'

Now he grinned again.

'Oh yes, we do – Sibylla.'

S he was dumbfounded at first. Her only clear thought was that things had gone badly wrong.

'How do you know my name?'

'I read the paper, like everyone else.'

He couldn't have recognised her – or could he? Not with her new hairdo, surely? A car drove past on the road outside and she looked at it over his shoulder through the kitchen window. Then it was gone.

'You might as well give up your idea of meeting Kerstin. She lives at the other end of town, as it happens. That house is empty. A German family has bought it and they usually don't turn up here until June.'

She wanted to get out of there, to get away from him.

'Why did you lock the door? What do you want from me?'

He didn't answer.

She glanced at the door again. There was no window in the hall.

'Don't even think about it, Sibylla. You're

going nowhere without my permission.'

She was a prisoner. She closed her eyes for a couple of seconds, trying to pull herself together. He moved away from the doorway and, because she had no choice, she followed him into the kitchen.

'I'd appreciate it if you took your shoes off.'

She stared at him. No fucking way.

Instead, she walked over to the table and sat down. A glance at him was enough to make her realise that keeping her shoes on had angered him a great deal. Frowning, he got hold of a brush and pan from a cupboard and started sweeping up invisible muck from the floor. When he had put the things away, he came to sit down at the kitchen table. The smile had gone from his face.

'From now on, you will do what I tell you.'

From now on? What was this weirdo after? Why was he so bossy?

She tried to speak in a low, calm voice.

'You have no right to keep me here.'

He grimaced with mock surprise.

'Oh, don't I? Dearie me. Maybe you'd like to phone the police?'

He burst out laughing when she didn't answer immediately. She told herself that maybe phoning the police was exactly what she should do now. They were both focusing on each other, registering each other's every breath. Another car went past and for a fraction of a second

Sibylla let her eyes wander away from him. He broke the silence.

'I must say, I was flabbergasted when you turned up in the cemetery out of nowhere. Like a gift from God. Indeed, God does look after his own.'

She stared at him.

'When I spotted your watch I couldn't believe my eyes at first. Do you know, if it hadn't been for your watch I might never have recognised you.'

They both looked at her watch. Then he smiled briefly before closing his eyes and turning his face upwards.

'Thank you Lord. You listened to your servant and saved my soul. You sent her to me. Thank you . . .'

She thought he had finished.

'What about my watch?'

He turned towards her, silent at first. His eyes were open but had narrowed to slits. Leaning over the table, as if to give his words more weight, he spoke slowly.

'Never ever interrupt me when I'm talking with the Lord God.'

Suddenly, everything fell into place.

'Accursed are those who rob the innocents of their rights.'

The truth pierced her like an arrow. Fear struck her speechless, her mouth filling with the taste of blood.

Fool that she was! What made all the difference was the person he had *appeared* to be. She already knew the importance of that for herself. How could she have forgotten? She had allowed prejudice to lead her by the nose – straight into a trap.

His face had changed somehow. Now he knew that she knew.

'You can guess where I saw that watch the first time, can't you? In the Grand Hotel's French dining-room. You were keeping Jörgen Grundberg company while he ate his last meal.'

A lert and quivering like tensed bow-strings, they sat watching each other across the kitchen table. Both were expecting something to happen that would release the tension. She lost any sense of time passing.

Trying to link isolated perceptions of the truth into a continuous chain, she began with him. She had been right, as well as catastrophically wrong. Rune Hedlund's secret was and was not what everyone had suspected. He had a lover, but the lover was a man.

Now, that man's strong hands were placed on the kitchen table in front of her. Hands which had carried out all the repulsive mutilations that she had been accused of. Stained with ordinary hobby paints and then covered with plastic gloves, they had searched the hidden cavities of his victims to recover what had been taken from his beloved's body.

She whispered an appeal to him.

'Tell me why.'

This made him relax and took them into a new phase of their relationship, in which neither needed to pretend to the other. There was no point in dropping hints or making covert threats. The only thing left between them was the final confrontation. Before that, she wanted to know and he wanted to tell.

Afterwards was another matter.

He seemed calm now, clasping his hands in his lap and poised, it seemed, ready to give a speech.

'Have you ever been to Malta?'

This question was so unexpected all the air went out of her, making a snorting noise. He might have thought she was laughing, because he started to smile again.

'I went to Malta. It was about six months after Rune's accident.'

The smile had faded from his face now, his hands were back on the table and he was looking down at them.

'No one ever grasped how . . . profoundly I mourned him.'

He inhaled deeply, as if needing more air before he could carry on speaking.

'Our love is buried in Rune's grave. They all pitied her, of course. People were trotting round to commiserate every hour God gave. Feeding her stuff they'd brought. Listening to her endlessly babbling on about how unfair life was. All her fucking garbage. There were times when I was on the brink of going there and shouting the truth out loud, straight into her fat, ugly face. I could've told her a thing or two! He had been with me that night, just before he collided with the elk. Straight from my bed, where my hands had held him and caressed him.'

Reaching out with his hands, stretching his long fingers, he wanted to make her feel what he felt. His terrible mental turmoil was almost palpable. He was on the verge of tears, his extended hands were shaking, his lungs struggling to get enough air and his lower lip trembling. His grief seemed mixed with barely restrained anger.

She reflected that this might well be the first time he had been free to put his feelings into words, the first time in the thirteen long months since Rune's death. The words had built up a pulsating pressure inside him, which was finally – maybe just this once – released.

'She went back to work soon enough. That meant she could be the queen of the coffee-room, droning on about how Rune's passing had not been in vain because she had been so generous with parts of his body, allowing four lives to be saved . . . blah, blah, blah.'

His head was shaking from side to side, his face twisted with disgust.

'Bullshit! It's enough to make you want to puke. Is that love? Is it? Letting them cut up the body you've loved? And then having his remains scattered to the four winds?'

He got up from the table, a movement so

sudden that she instinctively tried to back away. The wooden chair behind him tipped backwards and crashed on the floor. He righted it, walked across the kitchen to the sink, picked up the coffee-pot and came back.

'Would you like some more coffee?'

She shook her head, still in a state of confusion. He poured himself a cup and, with the same deliberation, took the pot back to the sink. She had calmed down enough to take the chance of looking around. Behind her was a closed door.

'After six months of this I thought I had better get away for a bit. Seeing her pious face every coffee break was becoming unbearable.'

The distance between where she was sitting and the door was about two metres.

'When I turned up there was only one reasonable holiday left at the travel agency. I didn't understand it then, but this was the first time the Lord showed me what he wanted me to do.'

By now he seemed more relaxed, pausing to drink mouthfuls of coffee and look out through the window. They must have looked quite idyllic – two old friends chatting together over a cuppa.

'The Malta trip was arranged by Leisure Tours, one of these group-travel firms. I didn't feel like being alone just then. Anyway, there's a cathedral city on Malta called Mosta and the Lord was guiding me to that sacred place.'

He had made fists of his hands now.

'You know, that excursion to Mosta changed my life. It was as if someone had pulled filters away from my eyes, allowing me to see the truth clearly for the first time.'

His face was glowing with gratitude.

'On the ninth of April in the year 1942, the cathedral was full of people, ordinary folk who had gone to Mass the way they always did. It was wartime. Suddenly, a bomb fell through the dome of the cathedral, shattering the splendid glass roof and burying itself in the floor of the aisle in front of the altar. Do you know, that bomb never exploded? God stopped the detonator functioning and the whole congregation completed Mass and left in safety. A true miracle!'

If he were expecting exclamations of wonder, he'd have to wait in vain.

'It was an English plane. Dropping the bomb was a mistake.'

His eyes were drilling into her.

'Don't you see what God was telling them?'

She shook her head.

'Their time hadn't come. God had not chosen to call anyone among the people in the church. They weren't meant to die just then. That's why He intervened to put the mistake right.'

He paused, looking at the window for a while.

'Rune was different, the Lord had called him.

I still don't know why. I'm waiting and praying for the Lord to tell me His reason. Maybe He will speak to me once my mission is complete.'

His confession was nearing its end and Sibylla felt fear returning, invading every part of her mind.

'She wouldn't let Rune die. She thwarted the will of God. She thought she could interfere with His power on Earth, trading parts of Rune's body and keeping them alive. It was trapping him halfway to Heaven. How could I allow that to happen?'

His face looked like a tragic mask. He clasped his hands.

'I will execute great vengeance upon them with wrathful chastisements. Then they will know that I am with the Lord, when I lay my vengeance upon them.'

In the silence that followed, Sibylla knew her will to act was still paralysed by fear. She needed more time.

'The people you killed – what about them? Had God called them too?'

He stared at her, his head to one side, apparently amazed by her question.

'What, haven't you understood that yet?'

She just looked back at him, not even daring to shake her head.

'The Lord had called them. They were meant to die. By what right do we hinder the acts of the Lord?'

She had no answer to that, of course. Telling him that he was stark staring mad would not be helpful.

'What about me?'

He smiled.

'You have been chosen.'

He made it sound like a compliment.

'The Lord is using you as one of His tools – like me. Both of us have been called to serve His ends.'

Soon, her time would be up.

'What's my task?'

The smile had widened to a grin that spread across his face.

'You're here to serve as my shield and protection.'

The next moment she was on her feet, throwing herself unhesitatingly backwards, grabbing the handle of the closed door behind her. Luckily for her it opened inwards and before he could get up and round the table, she was inside the room next door.

She was leaning her whole body against the door with frenzied strength, ready for him, when seconds later he started pushing at the handle from his side. She could feel his weight against the door. There was no key.

Looking around, she saw that the room was a painter's workshop, full of canvases and tubes of paint. There was an easel just behind her with an unfinished picture of the crucified Christ.

On the wall to her right was another door without a key.

Suddenly, she sensed that the pressure on the other side was no longer there. A quick glance through the keyhole confirmed it. He was gone.

She stepped back, hitting the corner of a table and knocking over a tin full of brushes.

It crashed to the floor. Terror sent electric currents through her body.

A sudden sound alerted her to his presence in the room to her right. He was going to use the other door. The next moment she saw his hand on the door frame and knew what she had to do. Taking one leap across the room, she threw her weight against the door, pinning his hand between it and the frame. She heard the crunching sound of something breaking in his squashed hand.

He did not scream, though his fingers extended in a spasm of pain. All she could hear was her own rasping, deep breathing, as if she were fighting for air.

There was a violent shove against the door, which opened it just enough to let him withdraw his hand. Then a clock on the wall next to her started striking the hour.

The sound unnerved her. She ran from the room, tore open the kitchen door and stood for a moment in the hall. The front door was locked, she knew. Running upstairs would take her deeper into the trap. A noise from next door meant that she had no more time. After taking a step forward she saw his feet and then the rest of him. He was sitting on the floor with his legs stretched out in front of him.

Quickly, she stepped past the open door and ran upstairs, hearing him get up. When she reached the landing three closed doors were

ᴈg her. One of them had a key in the lock.
. managed to unlock it in one go.

Then she heard him scream in real distress.

'Not in there!'

She was already inside by then and turning
the key in the lock with shaking hands.

The door handle was pushed down.

'Sibylla, don't do anything stupid!'

She turned to survey the room. An unmade
bed stood in the middle of the room. The
bed-linen must have been white once, but now
it was greyish and stained. A chest of drawers
with a mirror on top was placed against the
wall facing her. On it he had put a lit candle in
a magnificent silver candlestick. It was almost
two feet high and would have looked good on
a church altar. Next to it, was an open Bible.

'Sibylla! You must open this door! Immediately!'

She tried to open the window and was struggling to undo the hook. He heard the noise of
metal scraping against metal.

'Sibylla, don't open the window! The draught
will blow out the flame!'

His shouting had a note of desperation and
he was banging on the door.

She turned to look. True, the flame was
dancing in the draught from the open window.
Leaning out through the window, she realised
that the stone steps leading to the front door
were right below. If she jumped and managed to

avoid hitting the iron railings, she would almost certainly crack her head open on the steps.

He called again, sounding very stern.

'Sibylla, you must close that window.'

She left the window open and went to inspect the arrangement next to the mirror. Being in a locked room gave her a few precious moments to collect her thoughts.

Why was he so frantic about the candle?

Next to the candlestick lay two fresh candles, each as large as the burning one and still in its wrapper. There were also four unused long-lasting grave candles in white plastic containers.

She opened the Bible. On the inside of the stiff cover, someone had written a quote in careful script.

> For love is as strong as death
> Jealousy is as cruel as the grave.
> Its flashes are flashes of fire
> A most vehement flame.

Now she understood. Suddenly, the power-balance had shifted in her favour. The burning flame was her weapon.

She could hear something scratching in the lock. She called out loudly.

'If you come in I'll put the flame out!'

The sounds from the keyhole ceased.

'It has been burning since he died, hasn't it? Hasn't it?'

Not a sound from outside the door. It didn't matter, because now she knew. He had kept this flame burning, like the Olympic fire, as a living memory of his beloved.

She had gained more time. But for what? She looked around the room again.

It was empty apart from the bed and the chest of drawers. The floor was covered in a wall-to-wall brown carpet, with a couple of small rugs on top. Could she tie the sheets on the bed together to make a long enough rope to reach the ground? And then what? He could easily catch up with her, on foot or in the car.

Lifting the candlestick very gently, because that flickering flame was her shield, she called to him again.

'You can come in now!'

'You'll have to unlock the door.'

'I will, but you must count to three before entering. If you don't, I'll blow it out.'

No response. The carpet silenced her steps as she walked over to the door. She quickly turned the key in the lock and backed away. Three seconds later the handle was pressed down.

They stood facing each other, separated by the burning candle.

There was no mistaking the fury in his eyes. He stretched out his damaged hand and, when he looked down at it, her eyes followed his. A deep score ran across all his fingers and half the little finger seemed torn off. In the stillness, only the flame was moving.

Then he finally spoke.

'Why are you doing this? What do you hope to gain?'

'I want you to phone the police.'

He shook his head, not so much in refusal but to show his irritation.

'Don't you see we were meant to do what we've done? You and I are the elect. There's nothing we can do about it. The police don't matter. Put that candle down now.'

She didn't move, just sighed. Her breath made the flame flicker from side to side. The sight was an unwelcome reminder of how fragile her defence was. Instantly, a wave of paralysing terror rolled over her.

Perhaps he saw it in her face, perhaps he could smell her fear. He smiled slowly.

'We're of a kind, you and I. I've read about you in the papers.'

How could she get out?

'They've been getting one of your old mates from school to talk about you. Did you read that?'

The flame would die the moment she got outside. It could only protect her inside the house.

'I used to be a loner too . . .'

'Where's your telephone?'

'I was different from the start, even in primary

school. We are special, both of us, it's obvious to everyone . . .'

'Turn around. Walk downstairs, now. Or else, I'll blow.'

His smile disappeared, but he didn't move.

'I see. And tell me, Sibylla – then what will you do?

She said nothing. An eternity seemed to pass. Just when she thought her pounding heart would burst through her ribcage, he turned and walked downstairs. Slowly, she followed a few feet behind him, unsuccessfully attempting to control her breathing. She was holding her hand up to protect the flame and he was still extending his broken hand. Both moved one step at a time, the woman with the candle following the man, as if in a strange ceremonial procession.

She tried to think ahead. Would she tell him to phone? Should she do it herself? Four steps left. He had stopped at the bottom of the stairs.

'Walk on.'

He did as he was told and disappeared into the kitchen.

The silver candlestick was becoming heavy in her hand and she had to lower it. Now she too was standing on the floor of the hall.

He was out of sight.

'Come to the door!'

No movement in the kitchen. She changed hands.

'I'll blow it out!'

But by now it was clear to both of them that this was an empty threat. Once the flame was extinguished, she could do nothing. Then she would be completely in his power.

She walked through a door opposite the kitchen door. It led into a sitting room, carpeted with the same material as the upstairs bedroom. There was a sofa with an occasional table in front of it. No telephone anywhere.

On the wall to her left was the door leading into the workshop. It was slightly open. Her arm had become tired and she had to hold the candlestick with both hands now. Not a sound from the kitchen.

'Come out so I can see you!'

Still no reply.

She walked into the workshop, closing the door behind her. There it was, a grey Cobra set spattered with paint in every colour of the rainbow. The dial was underneath the receiver, which meant she had to use both hands. Watching the door to the kitchen, she carefully put the candlestick down, got hold of the receiver and began dialling with shivering fingers. Fear invaded her body, causing an almost physical pain. So near, yet so far from help.

Then he came at her.

Roaring, he tore open the door to the sitting room and before she could react, beat her to the floor with a kitchen chair. The pain made the world go dark. A moment later he was sitting astride her and she knew that one of her ribs was broken.

He was hissing with rage.

'Don't ever do that again!'

Trying to keep the pain away from her mind, she just shook her head.

'The Lord is with me. You cannot get away.'

She shook her head again. Anything to make him get up. Anything to stop him sitting on her ribcage.

He looked around.

'Stay on the floor!'

She nodded. At last, he left her alone. His first move was to take a cloth from the table and wind it tightly round his injured hand. She wondered if he was right-handed, because if so he would be really handicapped. Not as handicapped as she was, though. That fucking candle was still alight. She hadn't even managed to extinguish it.

What a bloody awful, shitty mess. And she had been so close.

She tried to twist a little to find a position where the pain would ease. Her jacket had balled up just where the pain was focused. He saw her move and put his foot on her stomach.

'Stay still!'

The pain was so intense she couldn't breathe, and her face contorted. She saw flashing stars under her eyelids before she blacked out. A moment later she opened her eyes again. He had taken his foot away, but was standing close to her, stretching out his damaged hand and raising the other. His face was deathly white. The raised hand was gripping a crucifix, which she had seen before. It was in one of the images among Patrik's print-outs.

He suddenly let it fall on her stomach.

'All yours!'

The crucifix wasn't heavy, but she instinctively tensed her stomach muscles as it fell and a new wave of pain flowed through her.

'You carry it yourself. It's your walk to Golgotha.'

If she had been able to speak, she might have asked what he meant.

'Get up now. We're going outside.'

S he managed to get up from the floor somehow. He grabbed her round the neck with
his good hand and forced her to walk bent
over, her eyes fixed on the floor and holding
the crucifix in her left hand.

Darkness was falling outside.

The pain in her chest was less intense when
she stood upright. Still grasping her neck, he
pushed her ahead of him down the steps.

'Where are we going?'

Silently, he kept shoving her on towards the
road. In her confusion, she thought that if she
really were a member of the elect, God would
surely send a car along this way.

He did not. Instead they crossed the road.
They were almost there when she realised where
they were going. The yellow house belonging to
the Germans.

'What's going to happen in there?'

'You're going to kill yourself.'

She tried to straighten up but he pushed her
head down again.

'They'll find you when they arrive in June.

The crucifix will be on your stomach. Everyone will realise what's happened, the jigsaw will be complete. At last, Sibylla will have atoned for her crimes. Kerstin will be able to identify you and I'll be standing by her, a loving support as always.'

They arrived at the steps leading to the front door. Sibylla pushed her right hand in her pocket. It curled round what she found there. Her nail file. Her fingers gripped the plastic handle.

The grip round her neck disappeared.

'I've got the keys in my pocket. My right jacket pocket. Pull them out.'

She straightened up and turned towards him. Their eyes met for a moment. Then she violently pushed the nail file into his face.

She did not stay to watch the result. When he put his hands to his face, she ran. The forest began on the other side of the low wooden fence and she leapt over it, somehow not feeling the pain in her chest.

He hadn't screamed this time either.

She kept up her speed. Sharp branches were whipping against her face as she pushed through the packed firs. The evening was still too light for her to hide. She must keep running and get away, far away. Before he came for her.

She did not know how long she had been running for, stumbling over stones and splashing through puddles in low-lying, swampy ground. By now she was wet up to her thighs and exhausted. She suddenly fell forward over something unrecognisable in the dark. Lying on the ground, her breathing was drowning all other sounds, her lungs burning with effort. Now and then she tried to stop panting, to hold her breath for long enough to listen to the forest.

At first, she heard only the wind in the trees. It was a gentle sound compared with the roaring of herself struggling for air. She just lay there for what felt like a long time. Still, but always watchful.

How badly had she hurt him? She wasn't safe yet, no way.

Then, suddenly, she heard his voice. It wasn't close, but it cut through the gathering dark far too distinctly.

'*Sibylla . . . you can't hide, not from us . . . God sees and hears everything . . . you know that . . .*'

Terror struck again.

Then the moon suddenly shone brightly on her. Like a heavenly lamp.

There was a fir with protective trailing branches in front of her. She quickly crawled into its dark shade.

'*Sibylla . . . where are you . . . ?*'

His voice sounded much closer. Her breathing was still treacherous.

Now, she could actually see him. He was

walking straight towards her hiding place, as
if he had been following an invisible thread
through the labyrinth of trees.

*'I know you're here . . . you must be here . . .
somewhere . . .'*

Now, she could see his face. It was covered
in blood. One wide-open eye was gleaming
white.

Fifty feet . . . thirty feet . . .

Then, in one blessed instant, the moon disappeared behind a cloud. She was saved. She
heard him groan, realising that he'd stumbled
and had tried to hold himself upright using his
wounded hand.

Serves you fucking right! You insane cunt!

She smiled. The disappearance of the moon
gave her hope again. She wasn't doomed to lose
this battle. For a while, he had almost made her
believe she had lost.

*'You haven't got a hope . . . sooner or later
we'll find you . . .'*

His voice was more distant now. Just for that
moment she was safe.

Perhaps she fell asleep on and off. She couldn't
be sure. The darkness was so dense that she
couldn't tell if her eyes were open or closed.
When dawn broke and the first glimpses of
contours became clearer, she crawled out from
her hiding place to try to find a road.

She couldn't go back, but then there was no

telling how far the forest stretched ahead. She decided to try to keep at a right angle to her first escape route. She should reach the road sooner or later, but well away from his house.

She was frozen, shivering with cold. Now that she had time to herself, the pain came back to haunt her. The broken rib ached angrily with each step.

The light was getting stronger every minute. Around her the forest was thinning. Tall, bare pine trunks rose around her, with hardly any undergrowth. He could see her easily here. Surely she would reach the road soon.

She heard a branch crack and stopped, trying to locate the sound. Another crack now, but from a different direction.

Then she saw them. One of them shouted at her.

'Lie down!'

He was in uniform and aiming at her with his handgun, gripping it with both hands. If she hadn't been so scared, she would have felt pure happiness to see them. She had never thought that she would be so utterly delighted at being surrounded by policemen.

She did as she was told, lying down, face against the ground, moving cautiously to mini-mise the pain. When she turned her head to look, four armed policemen were approaching her, all aiming their guns at her. She tried to speak to them.

'I don't know where . . .'

'Shut up! Just don't fucking move!'

Then, in one dizzying insight, she knew what had happened.

One of them pushed her face into the mossy ground, another frisked her body. One of them hissed at her.

'Murdering bitch!'

So he had got there first, ahead of her again.

S he obeyed orders, keeping her mouth shut
  during the whole journey to Vimmerby
police station. When she stepped out of the
car, a camera flashed in her face. When she
could see again, she caught a glimpse of a
young man with an enormous camera in front
of his face. Somebody asked her a question.

'Why did you do it?'

She was not given a chance to answer. Hard
hands pushed her into the entrance hall of the
police station. The whole room was full of people, civilians and uniformed staff, all observing
her closely, with disgust in their eyes.

'Move along. This way.'

The man who had been sitting next to her
in the back of the car was now walking ahead,
forming a small passage though the crowd.
Someone pushed her from behind, hitting the
broken rib. She grimaced with pain. A door
opened and she stepped through it.

'Sit down.'

She obeyed, pulling back the chair with her
handcuffed hands. Two men came in and sat

down behind the desk. One of them introduced himself.

'Roger Larsson.'

His colleague pushed a red button on a tape-recorder and checked that it was recording. Then he nodded.

'Interrogation of Sibylla Forsenström on the third of April 1999, starting at 8.45 a.m. Present in the room are the charged woman, Sergeant Mats Lundell and Inspector Roger Larsson.'

Larsson turned to her.

'You are Sibylla Forsenström?'

She nodded.

'I must insist that you answer every question loudly and clearly.'

'Yes, I am.'

'Tell us what you are doing in Vimmerby.'

She stared at the moving wheels in the tape-recorder, while they observed her intently. Someone knocked briskly on the door and a woman came in carrying a sheet of paper, which she handed to Roger Larsson. He read it quickly and put it away on the desk, text-side down. Then he looked at her again.

'I didn't do it.'

'Didn't do what?'

The question had been immediate. She was very tired and hungry. Her thoughts seemed to go all over the place. Now she had led them on to the right track.

'It's the man called Ingmar who's the murderer.'

The two men exchanged knowing glances, almost smiling at each other.

'Do you mean Ingmar Eriksson? A hospital porter, resident here in Vimmerby. He was hospitalised last night, after turning up in casualty with his right hand crushed and a nail file stuck in one eye. Is that the Ingmar you've got in mind?'

By the end of all this, he sounded angry. She looked down at her hands. If she moved them to hide the chain between them, the cuffs looked like two silver bracelets. The man called Roger was putting an object on the table in front of her.

'Why did you carry this about in your jacket pocket?'

Inside a plastic bag was the crucifix. She found it hard to speak.

'He gave it to me. He was going to murder me.'

'Why?'

'To make me take the blame.'

'Blame for what?'

She sighed.

'Everything. He had a relationship with Rune Hedlund.'

One corner of Roger Larsson's mouth was twitching.

'Who?'

'Rune Hedlund. He died in a car accident on the fifteenth of March last year.'

The men exchanged glances again. Neither said anything, but she realised what they were thinking. This woman was obviously deranged. Maybe they were right.

Moon or no moon, God had never been on her side.

'Phone Patrik. He knows that I didn't do it.'

'Who is Patrik?'

'Patrik . . . eh . . .'

She could not remember his surname. It had been on the door to their flat, but the memory had faded.

'His mother is in the police. They live on Sågar Street. South End.'

'South End in Stockholm – is that what you mean?'

Another knock on the door. The same woman came in with a new piece of paper. There were two curious faces peering in through the door behind her. Roger Larsson read what was on the paper, nodded and checked the time.

'Interrogation stopped at 9.03 a.m.'

Sibylla closed her eyes.

'We'll have a break now. Do you want to wait here or in a cell?'

She could barely keep her eyes open. Her whole being felt exhausted.

'Is there a bed in the cell?'

'Yes.'

'The cell, please.'

Hours passed without anything happening. The bunk was hard and she slept only in fits and starts. One longer period of sleep was more like a restless semi-conscious state, marred by obsessive dreaming about being chased and desperately trying to escape in slow motion from an invisible enemy.

They gave her food, but no one told her what they were all waiting for. She was too tired to ask. She was less troubled by the locked door than she had feared. It was actually quite nice just to lie there, freed from all responsibility. She had done her best, really done very well, if truth be told. But she had failed and all she could do now was accept her failure. They had won and she had lost.

That was all there was to it.

Later that afternoon, Roger Larsson came to see her. He told her that they were waiting to hear from the National Criminal Investigation Bureau in Stockholm. She had nothing to say to that. It seemed that she was considered

such a hardened criminal that she was outside the remit of the pathetic little Vimmerby
force. The elite team was coming to the res-
cue.

'You have the right to request a solicitor.'

'I haven't done anything wrong.'

He shrugged and went to the door.

'I think you'd better change your tune.'

Then he left her alone.

A little later, a man in his fifties came to see her.
He seemed agitated, either terrified or under
great stress. He dumped his briefcase on the
table in the cell.

'My name is Kjell Bergström.'

She sat up, but her face contorted with pain.
Her broken rib was announcing that it would
rather she stayed horizontal.

'I'm your legal adviser until further notice.
They'll presumably move you to Stockholm
soon, and find you someone else to help you
there. Your father is dead, did you know that?'

She stiffened.

'What did you say?'

Kjell Bergström pulled a sheet of paper from
his briefcase.

'This is a fax that's just come in from a
colleague in Vetlanda. They heard the news
that you had been captured.'

She responded quickly.

'I didn't do it.'

He lost his bustling show of efficiency and looked at her for the first time.

'It was a heart attack. Two years ago.'

Heart attack. Sibylla tested what it felt like. It didn't seem to matter in the slightest to her that Henry Forsenström had been dead for two years. As far as she was concerned, he had been dead for a very long time.

'My contact Krister Ek, the executor and a very good man, tells me that your mother, Beatrice Forsenström, believed for years that you were dead. When your father died, she appealed to have you declared officially dead. It was just about to be passed when you got in the news as wanted by the police.'

Sibylla realised that she was smiling. The corners of her mouth were irresistibly pulled upwards, even though there was no real reason.

'She thought I was dead, did she? So that was why she kept sending me fifteen hundred kronor every month for the last fifteen years? To this dead person?'

It was Kjell Bergström's time to be surprised.

'Did she, indeed?'

'Until last week.'

'Remarkable. Quite . . . remarkable.'

Yes, isn't it?

Bergström studied his fax again.

'As you surely know, your father had quite considerable assets. He left an inheritance that according to the law must be divided equally

338

between his spouse and any direct descendants. On the face of it, it's hard to escape the conclusion that your mother has been attempting to deprive you of your share.'

Sibylla felt like laughing out loud. Something was breaking inside, pushed apart by feelings that wanted release. She tried to control herself, burying her face in her hands and letting soundless laughter shake her body.

'I understand this must be difficult for you.'

Sibylla peered at him between her fingers. So, he thought she was weeping. Poor man, he was standing there utterly nonplussed by the problem of dealing with a serial killer, who was crying because her father had died. It made her want to laugh again. Her rib was aching dreadfully, causing tears to come to her eyes. When she sensed that her eyes were overflowing, she pulled herself together sufficiently to risk taking her hands away from her face.

He felt he had better try to comfort her.

'You mustn't worry. The law is on your side.'

This was too much. Her control cracked and new laughter welled up. She made snorting noises, holding her hands to her sides to dampen the pain.

The law was on her side!

She had just become a millionaire, but she would go straight into prison to serve life for four brutal murders, which she had not committed.

Presumably God was pleased with His handiwork – if He was looking her way, that is. Now
He and Ingmar could relax and live together
happily ever after, just contemplating their successes from time to time.

The laughter was dying away now, as suddenly as it had emerged. Left behind was only
a great empty space inside her.

He was observing her nervously.

'How do you feel?'

She looked up at him, with the tears still
streaming down her face.

How did she feel? Fucking awful. Everything
was fucking awful.

She laid down again, turning her back to him.
He went to the door and knocked to be let out.
He was away for a few minutes, but then she
heard the door opening and he returned.

'I'll stay with you just now. They'll be back
soon to take you in for further questioning.'

They did come soon afterwards. The pain when
she got up showed on her face. Bergström had
been watching her.

'Are you in pain?'

She nodded.

'Someone broke a chair on my ribcage.'

He asked no more questions. Maybe this kind
of thing was common practice in Vimmerby?

She obediently reached out her hands towards

the policeman, expecting to be handcuffed again, but he only shook his head.

The interrogation room was empty when they came in. She sat down on the same chair and Kjell Bergström stood, leaning against the wall. One man and one woman came in soon afterwards, new people this time. Bergström shook hands with them, but Sibylla stayed where she was. Presumably she didn't need to introduce herself.

Three pairs of eyes were watching her. The unknown man spoke first.

'How are you feeling?'

She couldn't be bothered answering and just smiled a little.

'My name is Per-Olof Gren. I'm working for the National Criminal Bureau. This is my colleague Anita Hansson.'

Bergström went back to lean against his wall, while the newcomers settled behind the desk. No one started the tape recorder.

'We had hoped that you would feel strong enough to tell us about what happened last night.'

Feel strong enough? What was this soft approach meant to achieve? Sibylla sighed and leaned against the back of the chair. Thoughts were tumbling about inside her head. It seemed impossible to arrange any of them in an orderly sequence.

She stared at the desktop.

'I was in the cemetery. I met Rune Hedlund's widow. Ingmar turned up afterwards and I went away with him.'

'Is he the person who beat you up?'

She looked up.

'Yes, he is. With a chair. I think one of my ribs is broken.'

'What about the scratches on your face?'

'I got them when I was running away from him. Through the forest.'

The man looked at his woman colleague.

'You were lucky, you know.'

Oh, yeah? Super-lucky is the word.

Suddenly, Anita Hansson spoke up.

'I believe you know Patrik.'

A small ray of hope was coming through the thick cloud of dejection.

'Did you find him?'

'He's my son.'

Sibylla stared at her. Patrik's mum, she who was 'in the force'. Nothing in Anita Hansson's face revealed her feelings about the matter.

'This morning, when the news broke, he told me all about it.'

For a moment, Sibylla thought she was dreaming.

'I phoned the National Bureau once I'd convinced myself that he was telling the truth. It all hung together, except the name Thomas Sandberg, of course. A bit confusing, that.'

'I wanted to keep Patrik away from the case at that stage. He had helped me enough, I thought.'

Patrik's mother nodded. She clearly thought so, too.

Per-Olof Gren began to explain.

'We searched Ingmar Eriksson's house this morning. He kept the . . . remains in his fridge.'

'. . . *What a shame. I've forgotten about the shopping. I'm afraid you'll have to be content with just coffee, after all.*'

Again, self-defence came first.

'I didn't put them there.'

Per-Olof Gren spoke soothingly.

'Sibylla, calm down. We know it wasn't you.'

She scarcely dared to believe her ears. This couldn't be true. Not now, when she had finally accepted her fate.

'He has confessed. He cracked when we found the glass jars in his fridge. He was going to bury the lot in Hedlund's grave.'

The room was silent. Sibylla was trying to get her mind round this completely new situation, but she was far too tired to manage.

'It would have been helpful if you had come to us a little earlier. We could have avoided all this.'

This was Patrik's mother speaking again. Sibylla understood only too well what she meant. Her inner ear was tuned in to the row Patrik had been given.

She looked at them, speaking quietly.

'You wouldn't have believed me. Or would you?'

No one replied.

'Only Patrik did. Maybe he is the only one who has trusted me. Ever.'

A long silence. Per-Olof finally broke it.

'Well, there you are. You're free to go. What do you plan to do?'

Bergström stepped away from his wall.

'I know what Miss Forsenström is doing next. She's coming with me to Vetlanda. We're going to have a little talk with her mother.'

Sibylla shook her head.

'No. I can't face her.'

'Sibylla, I don't think you know what you're saying.'

'I want 300,000 kronor. That's all I need.'

Bergström smiled condescendingly.

'My dear Sibylla, we're talking many millions here.'

Their eyes met and, after a while, it seemed that he had almost accepted that she meant it.

'But you shouldn't let her get away with it. She's keeping back an entire fortune.'

Sibylla thought about a fortune, but couldn't imagine what she would do with it.

'OK. Seven hundred grand. Tell her where to put the rest, why don't you?'

The lock whirred, even before she had time to take her finger off the bell. She wondered if he always stood next to the buzzer. Just like the last time, he was waiting by his open front door when she reached his landing. Neither of them spoke before she'd stepped inside and he'd pulled the door shut behind them.

'You've done well – from notorious serial killer to popular heroine in just one week. It's impressive, no other word for it.'

She walked into the room, straight to his computer. This time he did not stop her.

'Did you find him?'

He nodded.

'How much did you say you wanted this time? Five grand?'

He smiled. She put her hand in her jacket pocket, found the notes and put them down on the keyboard. He pulled a white envelope out of the back pocket of his jeans and handed it to her.

'Your kid, is he?'

She just looked at him, took the envelope and

walked away from him, in the direction of the hall. He followed her.

'Can't help being curious.'

She didn't reply, just went out on the landing and closed his front door behind her. This was the first time that she allowed herself to think about it and give way to her feelings. She was shaking all over. To calm herself, she walked down one floor. Only then could she contemplate even looking at the envelope. She sat down on a step, her heart beating hard.

The white envelope contained the answer to fourteen years of anxious speculation.

Who was he? Where did he live? What kind of person was he?

Now she would know.

The bus was leaving in two hours' time. The documents had been signed and exchanged, the cheque was on the table. They had arranged for Gunvor Strömberg to meet her in the bus terminal to hand over the keys.

Peace and quiet. Rest for a troubled soul.

In this white envelope was the name of the one who had always been missed.

She would always miss him. She had lost him fourteen years ago and now, everything she could do was too late – far too late.

Why was she doing this? For his sake? Or for her own sake?

She stopped walking downstairs, struck by her own unexpected insight into his rights, as opposed to hers.

So, by which right would she come marching into his life, fourteen years after his birth? What did he have to gain? She would get the reward of knowing, of her search having come to an end. Did he owe her that?

He was free from grief. Why should she drag him along to share hers?

If she still owed him anything, it was to bear her sense of loss on her own.

She had arrived on a landing. On the wall in front of her was the lid to a rubbish chute. People stopped there to throw their bags of waste into the basement bin. A useful place to shed your past. Her heart pounding in her chest, she opened the lid. She did not feel anxious. Her mind was filled with the liberating knowledge of doing the right thing.

If the bus service stuck to the timetable, she would be home in time to hear her neighbour's trumpet play a greeting to the setting sun.